"*Tuck! Everyone will see!*" Adrienne glanced at the other people on the beach.

"*I want everyone to know that you're my girl!*"

"*Tuck!*"

"*Are you saying that you won't be my girl?*"

"*No. But it's all happening so fast! You don't give me a chance to think!*"

"*It's happening fast for me too, Adrienne, but please don't tell me I'm wrong.*" His tone changed. "*I'm not, am I? I know I'm not the smartest person in the world, and too often I open my mouth before my brain is in gear, but I'm right this time, aren't I?*"

"*Yes, Tuck,*" Adrienne answered. She leaned over to kiss him. Tuck moved closer and put his arms around her. She leaned her head against his shoulder.

Dear Readers:

Thank you for your unflagging interest in First Love From Silhouette. Your many helpful letters have shown us that you have appreciated growing and stretching with us, and that you demand more from your reading than happy endings and conventional love stories. In the months to come we will make sure that our stories go on providing the variety you have come to expect from us. We think you will enjoy our unusual plot twists and unpredictable characters who will surprise and delight you without straying too far from the concerns that are very much part of all our daily lives.

We hope you will continue to share with us your ideas about how to keep our books your very First Loves. We depend on you to keep us on our toes!

Nancy Jackson
Senior Editor
FIRST LOVE FROM SILHOUETTE

ADRIENNE AND THE BLOB

Judith Enderle

First Love from Silhouette

Published by Silhouette Books New York

America's Publisher of Contemporary Romance

SILHOUETTE BOOKS
300 E. 42nd St., New York, N.Y. 10017

ISBN: 0-373-06174-9

First Silhouette Books printing February 1986

America's Publisher of Contemporary Romance

Printed in the U.S.A.

RL 5.3, IL Age 11 and up

First Love from Silhouette by Judith Enderle

Secrets #115
Adrienne and the Blob #174

JUDITH ENDERLE was born and grew up in Michigan. She now lives in California with her husband and their three teenage children. She has been writing ever since fourth grade, and published her first story in *Highlights* in 1978. Since then she has published many articles, short stories and novels. Admired for her clever plots and sense of humor, she often chooses as her themes the importance of communication and the joys and responsibilities of friendship.

Chapter One

At exactly seven-thirty Adrienne opened her eyes and pushed the button on her alarm clock before it rang. Why she bothered to set it, she didn't know. She couldn't remember the last time she'd heard that insistent jangle; she certainly didn't miss it. She always awoke at seven-thirty each morning. There was exactly enough time to feed the animals, eat breakfast, and get to school—even in the summer.

Thunder rumbled in the distance. She threw back her pale-yellow sheet and slipped from her bed. The air felt sticky.

In the corner, she uncovered her parakeet's cage. "Good morning, Tweetledum," she said.

The green-feathered bird flapped his wings and jumped from his perch to the wire on the side of the cage.

Tweetledum is an appropriate name all right, thought Adrienne, as she filled his cup with bird seed. Although he could squawk, this bird had never learned to say one word despite the hours she'd spent trying to teach him.

From the parakeet she moved to the table under her window and the cage that contained her guinea pig, Lancelot. When he was breakfasting, she turned to the fish aquarium and sprinkled dried food on the surface of the water. On her way outside to take care of the brown rabbits, Ding and Dong, she passed her mother's room. Her mom was still asleep. She'd worked the late shift at the restaurant where she was hostess and assistant manager. Adrienne didn't disturb her, but went on through the tidy apartment to the balcony.

When she'd put food in the rabbit house and scratched both bunnies behind the ears, she stood at the rail and looked over the cloud-shrouded city. Was there someone else way out there standing on a balcony and looking toward her? A sense of loneliness overcame her as it sometimes did on these isolated early mornings. She and Mom got along all right, and occasionally she saw Dad. Shelley was her friend, and of course there were the animals; but Adrienne felt as if there was something missing. She didn't know what. Her mother would say it was a boyfriend.

Adrienne shook herself. Feeling sorry for herself wasn't her normal habit. She was a doer. And she had to get doing, if she was going to be on time for the first session of the summer biology class. She was glad she'd been accepted by Mr. Garrison. His independent study class was hard to get into, and he accepted only a few students each summer. Last year there had been only three. The first fat drops of a summer storm fell as she closed the glass door behind her.

Adrienne was out of the shower, dressed in jeans and a pink T-shirt, and at the kitchen table eating when her mother emerged from her room.

"You look disgustingly wide awake, honey." She wrinkled her nose as she lifted a slat of the Venetian blind over the sink and peered out the window. "I hate rain."

Adrienne smiled. "I know, Mom. Maybe it will stop before you have to go to work."

"Maybe." Her mother turned the burner on under the kettle and sat in the chair across from Adrienne. She and her daughter were built alike—tall and trim. They both had shoulder-length blond hair with a hint of red running through it. The only difference was their eyes. Adrienne's eyes were clear-blue and searching. Her mother's were hazel and tired. Tiny lines like fingers stretched out from the corners.

"Were you busy last night?" Adrienne nibbled on the edge of a slice of toast.

"Mobbed. I walked my feet off. I think I'll ask Gary for a raise."

"When the restaurant's busy should be a good time to ask," said Adrienne.

Her mother nodded and stood to turn off the kettle that shrieked behind them on the stove. "What are your plans for today, honey?"

"My summer-school class starts this morning." Adrienne glanced up at the clock. "And I'd better hurry or I'll be late. I don't want to get tossed out before I begin."

"Summer-school biology. What will you study? Boys?"

Adrienne smiled. Her mother worried because she was sixteen and didn't date. "You never know, Mom." The phone rang as she carried her cup and plate to the sink. "I'll get it."

"Adie, this is Shelley. Want to do something today?"

"Mm-hm. Get to school on time," said Adrienne. In the background at the Warner house, she could hear the chaotic sounds of a big family breakfast. Her best friend had five brothers, one older and four younger.

"School," groaned Shelley. "We just got out of school. Why do you want to go during the summer?"

"I got accepted into Mr. Garrison's class; did you forget?"

"Yeah. I did. Now what am I going to do? If I don't get out of here fast, Mom will remember that it's summer and stick me with the little kids."

"Come with me, then we'll go someplace after—maybe the mall," Adrienne suggested, though she knew her friend was exaggerating. Being the only girl in a family of boys, gave her friend her own way more often than not. In fact, Shelley could even be considered slightly spoiled.

"Are you sure it will be okay? Mr. Garrison might not let me stay."

Adrienne could picture her friend biting her lip and struggling to make a decision. "Positive. We probably won't do much the first day, anyway."

A loud shout from Shelley's father brought a quick answer. "Okay. I'll meet you in front of school."

"See you there. Nine o'clock." Adrienne hung up the phone. "Shelly and I might . . ." she began.

"I heard. Take some money from my purse so you can buy something," said her mother. "You might look for a new bathing suit. That old all-purpose one you wear to sunbathe on the balcony has seen much better days."

"You're right. Thanks, Mom." Adrienne kissed her mother and ran to finish getting ready.

The rain was falling harder when she caught the eight-thirty bus. She'd be at school in plenty of time. There was no worry about being late. And there was no hope of meeting a lot of boys in this class. She doubted that any had signed up.

Shelley was waiting in front when Adrienne got off the bus. Her friend was sitting on the high-school-name sign, holding an umbrella over her head, and swinging her feet over the D of Pendleton High School. The moist wind blew her short brown hair away from her freckled face. She was gripping the umbrella as if she feared that, like Mary Poppins, she'd be lifted aloft into the clouds.

"You could have waited inside," Adrienne called. She pulled up the collar of her white nylon jacket and raced through the fat raindrops.

Shelly slipped off the sign and came to meet her. She handed the umbrella to Adrienne, who was the taller of the two girls but only by a couple inches. "I've seen enough of the inside of the school, thanks. I still don't know what made you sign up for Garrison's class. You never wanted to go to the special summer-school classes before."

"Garrison's class is different. He gives you the general assignment, then you're on your own. It will be like being a biologist, without teacher breathing down your neck. And it's an advanced placement class. I can get college credit."

"Sounds as if he has the good deal going. He gets vacation and paid to teach, too."

"I'm sure it's not like that. Someone will have to keep track of our research."

"Research, huh? Sounds spooky, Dr. Jekyll," said Shelley.

"Maybe you will be my experiment," said Adrienne, falling into the role.

"Not me. Although I might be interested in a new body, now that you mention it," said her friend.

"Alan thinks you look pretty good."

"Alan doesn't care what I look like. We're quits. Didn't I tell you?"

"No. When did that happen? Why didn't you call me?"

Adrienne collapsed the umbrella, then held the side door open for her friend. The halls were quiet in comparison to normal school time. There were a few students walking around and waiting outside class-rooms for the special offerings of summer, but like Shelley, most kids preferred to spend their vacation elsewhere.

"I couldn't talk about it. He told me last night that he didn't want to go out with me anymore. He said we were getting too serious." With the back of her hand, she brushed away several tears from the corners of her brown eyes.

Adrienne tucked the umbrella under her arm then patted Shelley's shoulder. "Hey, there are other guys."

"Sure. But none who will notice me."

"Someone will. Alan wasn't the right one for you, I guess."

"No. He thinks he's the right one for Margie Kent. If he thinks I was too serious, wait until he's gone out with her a few times. They don't call her spider lady for nothing."

"Never mind Margie. We'll do things together," said Adrienne. "Though my mother keeps bugging me, I don't date anyone."

"Yeah. Why? You could get a dozen boys."

"I don't want a dozen boys. One special boy, who has something in common with me, will be enough. I'll know him when he comes along."

"That's what I thought, too." Shelley blew her nose on a tissue she'd pulled from her pocket. "What room is the great class in?"

"The bio lab, of course," said Adrienne. "Upstairs."

"Of course. Lead the way. I never knew you were so interested in science."

"Not in any science. In biology. You know how I love animals. I might be a veterinarian. And biology is one of the classes I'd have to take." Adrienne turned at the staircase and started up. Her friend Shelley followed. There was no one waiting outside the lab when they got there.

"Do you suppose you're the only one taking the class?" Shelley's voice dropped to a whisper in the echoing hall.

"I don't know. Here comes Mr. Garrison. We'll find out in a minute."

The tall, gray-haired teacher strode down the hall. "Good morning, girls," he said.

"Good morning," they chimed together, like elementary school children.

Shelley put a hand over her mouth to stifle a giggle. They waited for Mr. Garrison to unlock the laboratory door. "Do you mind if my friend waits for me?" Adrienne asked, as they followed the teacher into the room.

"She can wait every day, if she wants; but I won't give her credit for the class."

"Oh, that's all right, Mr. Garrison," said Shelley.

"Isn't anyone else coming?" Adrienne perched on one of the stools behind the first lab table. Shelley sat next to her. The faint odor of formaldehyde lingered from school term dissections.

"There will be two of you this year." Mr. Garrison looked at his watch, just as Brad Ferris came through the door. "And here's your partner for this summer," said the teacher.

Brad looked intense, almost too serious, as if he carried the weight of the world on his shoulders. Though he was built like a football player, he didn't play sports. He'd been in several of Adrienne's classes, yet she didn't know him at all.

"Hi," said Adrienne.

Brad nodded and sat down at the opposite end of the table.

"The instructions for this class aren't complicated," said Mr. Garrison. "I'll give you one general assignment. You are to experiment, observe, make notes, and turn in a report to me on the first day of school. You may meet here in the lab to work; spend as much time as you need." He stepped from behind his desk and came over to the table. "Adrienne, here's the key to the classroom. It's up to you to see that Brad has access to the key on the days you aren't here and vice versa. Any questions?"

"You mean you won't be here?" Brad asked.

"I might check in once or twice. This is independent research. You don't need me to do it for you," said the teacher. "That's one of the reasons I'm selective about the students; not everyone can hack working on his own." Adrienne tucked the key in her jacket pocket then raised her hand.

"Yes, Adrienne."

"What's the general assignment?" she asked.

"I'm getting to that. Any other questions?"

"How long does the report have to be?" asked Brad.

"As long as you have to make it, to be thorough on the topic assigned. This is independent research. You may find something that Adrienne doesn't and vice versa."

"May I share information with Brad and—" Adrienne hesitated "—vice versa?"

Mr. Garrison didn't seem to notice that she'd picked up his word. "No problem. If you want to work as partners, that's acceptable, but you have to write separate papers. Anything else?"

Brad glanced at Adrienne. He didn't look as if he'd welcome a partner. She shook her head.

"Nothing?" said Mr. Garrison. "Fine. The assignment for this year is the study of life at Indian Vale Marsh, specifically swamp life found in the water, although other types of life may be included in your report."

"A spooky place, but interesting, Mr. G. I know several teachers and a few other people who probably call the place home," said a voice from the doorway.

Adrienne, Shelley and Brad turned to see who'd spoken.

Chapter Two

Tucker Michaels lounged in the doorway. Lanky in build, with dark curls, he was known as a clown with a good opinion of himself; everyone at Pendleton knew Tuck or who he was.

"Is he in this class, too?" asked Shelley.

"Are you dropping out if I am?" Tuck sauntered into the room and leaned against the corner of the table behind them. Half-sitting, half-standing, he grinned at the four people staring at him.

Shelley's face turned bright red. "I'm not in, so I can't," she said. "Otherwise..."

"Otherwise what? You'll go with me to dumbbell English?"

"I think you should return to your assigned class, Mr. Michaels," said Mr. Garrison.

"Aw, Mr. G., they aren't doing nothing."

"I can hear why he belongs there," muttered Brad.

"You say something?" Tuck went to lean on the table beside Brad. In his muscle T-shirt and faded jeans, he looked like a television-show character. Adrienne suspected that he was trying to act like one, too.

"Yeah. I said I can hear why you belong in dumbbell English," Brad said louder.

"Me, too," Tuck said with a grin. "Dumb, dong. Dumb, dong." He pointed to his head. "Sometimes I don't talk so good."

Shelley suppressed a giggle, and in spite of herself, Adrienne found herself smiling.

"Tucker," said Mr. Garrison.

"I'll go back tomorrow, Mr. G. They're handing out lists." He reached into his back pocket then held up a sheet of paper. "Now they're reading the list. I might not know my English, but I can read a stupid list."

"We're finished in here, Tucker," said Mr. Garrison. "I'll leave you, Adrienne and Brad, to plan your classes. I'll be back in about six weeks to pick up your preliminary reports. Your final drafts will be due when school starts again." He picked up his briefcase and left.

"You got to write reports?" asked Tuck. "Bummer and a half. I thought you just got to poke around in the swamp. You never know what creepy thing you might find living out there." He put his arm around Adrienne. "Oooo," he said in her ear. "I am the swamp creature."

"Quick! Write this down, Brad," said Adrienne. "Our first swamp life."

"Jerk," said Brad.

"What a specimen," said Shelley and blushed again.

"Oooo," said Tuck, descending on her and pretending to bite her neck.

Shelley squealed.

"We have some serious work to do," said Brad. "Would you quit playing the creep and please leave?"

"No, I will not, thank you," said Tucker with a mock British accent. "And watch what you call me, Ferris," he added in a normal voice. "This class sounds a lot more interesting than that dumbbell junk." He sat on a stool between Shelley and Brad.

"But don't you have to take that class?" asked Shelley.

"Tucker Michaels doesn't have to do anything. Besides, I know what they're going to do. I have all the info on this sheet of paper." He waved the paper at them. "I can do it at home."

"What about tests?" asked Adrienne.

"Half the class knows me. They'll clue me in, and I'll show up and pass the tests. Don't worry."

"Why did you end up in that class in the first place?" Adrienne asked.

"Cause I'm a dummy dingdong, don't ya know?"

"Sure," she said. "So I heard."

Tuck stared at her. She didn't look down or away, but stared right back. Finally he gave in with a shrug. "So, when are we going to the swamp?"

"You aren't," said Brad. "This is a serious class. We're serious students—at least I am," he added.

What's eating him? Adrienne wondered. He hasn't lightened up since he walked through that door. Brad wasn't a bad-looking guy, but with the log he was hauling around on his shoulder, no one would want to get close to him.

"I'm serious, too." Tuck sounded as if he meant it.

"You really want to come?" asked Adrienne.

"I really want to," said Tuck. Again his gaze locked with hers.

This time she looked away.

"What about me?" asked Shelley.

"You can come, too," said Adrienne.

Brad slammed his notebook shut. "And when is this party taking place? I have a report to write."

"So do I," snapped Adrienne. "I suggest we meet here tomorrow morning, then go to the swamp to observe and take the first water samples. I'll ask my mom if I can use her car."

"Sounds fine with me. See you guys tomorrow, then." Tuck jumped off the stool, then swung out the door as quickly and as quietly as he'd entered.

"You're going to be sorry you encouraged him," said Brad. "He isn't serious, you know."

"We'll see," said Adrienne. "Do you want to work together or separately?"

Surprisingly, Brad didn't answer immediately. She'd expected a definite "separately."

"Let's decide after we go to the swamp," he said.

Adrienne zipped her jacket. She felt the pocket for the key. "We'll meet here in the morning. Eight-thirty," she said.

Brad nodded, then left the room.

"What's the matter with him?" whispered Shelley.

"Who knows?" Adrienne shrugged. "Were you serious about coming with us to the swamp?"

"Are you afraid to go alone with Brad?" Shelley asked teasingly.

"Hah! You have to be kidding. Now with Tuck, that might be a different story."

"He is cute," said Shelley.

"And he knows it," said Adrienne. "Big ego."

"Still, there's something appealing about him, wouldn't you agree?"

"I didn't notice."

"Sure you didn't."

"I don't know what you're talking about. Come on. Let's go to the mall. I'm starved."

"It's not even ten o'clock."

"I ate a small breakfast."

"You're changing the subject, Adie. You like Tucker Michaels."

Adrienne went ahead of her friend out the lab door. She checked to be sure the door locked behind them.

"Adie," Shelley said in a singsong voice.

"What?" Adrienne pretended she didn't know what her friend was talking about.

"You do like Tuck, don't you?"

"I don't know him. I guess he's okay."

"Well, I like him. But he didn't look at me the way he looked at you."

"Shelley, your imagination is overworking."

"Adie, my friend, this is one place where I've had more experience than you. Guys have certain looks they give girls. And the look Tucker Michaels gave you said he was interested."

"He can be interested all he wants. That doesn't mean I feel the same."

They clattered down the stairs. Adrienne ran toward the exit with Shelley at her heels. If she ran, she didn't have to talk about Tuck. She remembered the way they'd stared at each other, and each time she thought about it, her heart did beat a bit too fast. But she was waiting for a boy with whom she'd have something in common. And she couldn't think of one thing she and Tucker Michaels had in common—well maybe one: their last names both began with the letter M. But that certainly wasn't enough to make her think twice about him.

"Let's forget about Tuck and Brad and the class," she said. "I want to try on bathing suits. I need a new one."

"What for? To wear to Indian Vale Marsh?" Shelley asked.

They stepped out into the humid air and gray day. The rain had stopped but there was definite promise of more to come.

Adrienne swatted her friend with the umbrella. They both laughed, then ran again—this time to catch the bus to the mall.

They bought ice-cream cones and walked past the shop windows, pointing to the outfits they'd buy if they were rich. After finishing the cones, Adrienne tried on ten different bathing suits before choosing a dark-green bikini, which Shelly told her made her look like a water nymph.

"Perfect for the swamp," said Adrienne.

"I didn't say that, you did," returned her friend.

"How about a fat, juicy hamburger?" asked Adrienne when they left the store.

"At Fat and Juicy's? Let's go." Shelley led the way to the hamburger stand hidden at the far end of the mall. They carried their food to a table and sat down to eat and people-watch.

"Oh, oh," said Shelley.

"What's the matter?" Adrienne wiped her mouth with a napkin and turned to look in the direction her friend was staring. Brad Ferris was coming their way.

"Shall we blend with the crowd?" asked Shelley, grabbing for hamburger wrappers.

"No. Odds are he'll walk by as if he doesn't know us. Look at how he's frowning."

"Thunder in person."

To Adrienne's surprise, Brad stopped at their table, pulled up a chair and sat down.

"Small world," said Adrienne.

Shelley raised her eyebrows as if to say "I knew we should have left."

"Yeah. Listen, I really don't think we should let Tucker Michaels go with us tomorrow."

"Hi, Brad," said Shelley.

"Did you hear what I said, Adrienne?" He gripped the edge of the table and leaned forward.

"And did you hear what I said?" Shelley asked. "Can't you even say hello? What's with you, anyway?"

"What do you mean?"

"You don't jump right in with orders," said Shelley. "You didn't even say hello."

"Oh. Well, I've been thinking about Michaels ever since I left school."

Shelley glanced at Adrienne, who looked away from her friend.

"So? You can still say hello," insisted Shelley.

"All right. Hello. Now, about Michaels—"

"Don't worry about him. He'll get bored after one trip, if he even shows up, then go back to dumbbell English," Adrienne said.

"The guy gets under my skin," said Brad.

"Why?" asked Shelley.

"Why. Start with Jenny Forester."

"Jenny Forester? I know who she is, but I don't know her," said Adrienne.

"Neither do I, anymore," said Brad.

"Is she your girlfriend?" Shelley asked.

"Was," said Brad.

"And is she going with Tuck now?" she asked.

"Someone just like him—a big-mouth know-it-all."

Shelley sighed. "I know how you feel. My boyfriend, Alan Burlington, broke up with me last night, and I can't believe who he's taking out now. It's the pits."

"You seem okay," Brad said.

"I have a friend to talk to." She glanced at Adrienne. "It helps, a little."

"I'm not that lucky." He ran his hands through his hair. He looked from Shelley to Adrienne and then back to Shelley. "You've been there and know what it's like. I had such a neat summer planned. She was even going to sign up for Mr. Garrison's class, but she changed her mind."

"I don't know what Alan's doing, but he's doing it with Margie," said Shelley. "We should get together, Brad."

She has to be kidding, Adrienne thought.

"Yeah. We should," he agreed. For the first time, Brad smiled. "Give me your phone number? I'll call you later."

"All right." Shelley gave him the number.

He jotted it on a slip of paper and put it in his wallet. "Well, I have to go. I'd still rather that Michaels didn't go to Indian Vale," he said.

"And I don't think we should make a big deal about it," said Adrienne.

Brad shrugged. "I'll call you later, Shelley," he said. Then he left.

"You're in for it, now," said Adrienne, stirring the ice in her cup with a straw.

"No, I'm not. Why?"

"He's a jerk. You were the one who wanted to run when you saw him coming."

"That was before I understood his problem."

"He's got more than one. I bet he'll spend all the time crying about Jenny or complaining about Tucker."

"So it's Tucker now."

"Shelley, you know what I mean. You heard him."

Shelley nodded. "You can't know what breaking up is like, Adie. I don't think he's as bad as he seems. Underneath he might be a nice guy. He's hurting right now. Boys have feelings, too, you know."

"All right. All right. Don't get so defensive. Are you finished with your hamburger? I want to buy a notebook for my class."

"So you can write letters to Tucker?"

"Just because you have illusions about the kind of guy Brad is, don't think I have any about Tucker Michaels. He and I are nothing alike. We have nothing in common. Forget your crazy ideas.

"Oh, I will." Shelley gathered the papers from their lunch. "But you won't. I know the signs."

"You know nothing," said Adrienne. "Let's go home so you can wait for Brad to call and cry on your shoulder."

Chapter Three

The sun was shining and promising a beautiful day when Adrienne pulled the car into the drive beside the old white frame house, early the next morning. She jumped out and ran up the walk. Not bothering to knock, she opened the door and called, "Shelley, it's Adrienne. Are you ready?"

"Almost. I'm in the kitchen. Come on through."

The smell of fried bacon and fresh coffee made Adrienne's mouth water as she stepped inside. She passed through the living room where seven-year-old Toby and ten-year-old Sam were watching cartoons.

"Hi, Adie," said Toby.

"Hi," she said.

Sam didn't say anything.

In the bright blue kitchen, the table was still piled with breakfast dishes. Shelley was finishing her breakfast. Her mother was sorting clothes in the small laundry off to the side.

"Hi, everyone." Adrienne took the slice of bacon Shelley offered.

"Hi, Adie. How are you? How's your mother?" Mrs. Warner asked.

"She's fine. Busy. Tired."

Mrs. Warner nodded, as if she understood perfectly the conflicting statements that Adrienne had made.

"Are you ready, Shelley?"

"Mm-hm. I have to brush my teeth, then we can leave. Come on. You can wait in my room."

Adrienne followed Shelley upstairs. Her friend's room was pretty with pink-flowered wallpaper and white priscilla curtains. She had an iron daybed with a trundle that pulled out for overnight guests. Being the only girl in a family with all the boys had some advantages, Adrienne guessed. Shelley didn't always agree.

"Did Brad call you?" Adrienne sat on the edge of the bed.

"Jftamnt."

"What?"

"I said, just a minute. My mouth was full of toothpaste. Yes, he called me."

"And?"

"And nothing. He talked about Jenny, and I talked about Alan. Did Tuck call you?"

"Of course not. Why should he?"

"Oh, I thought he might."

"You thought wrong. Hurry up, Shelley."

"I'm hurrying. Let's go." Shelley grabbed her purple sweat shirt from the closet. "Come on, Adrienne. Don't sit there dreaming about Tuck."

"I'm not. And I want you to lay off on all this Tuck business."

"Ooh. Touchy. All right. I won't mention his name." She called over her shoulder as they went down the stairs.

"Good. Take your boots. The marsh is muddy."

"Right. I forgot." Shelly pulled her boots from the downstairs hall closet.

"Have a nice time today, girls," called Mrs. Warner. She hurried past them as Shelley opened the front door. She was on her way to answer the sleepy-sounding call from upstairs. Shelley's littlest brother, Rory, was awake and wanted to get out of his crib. The two boys missing that morning were Ethan, who was at camp, and Bill who was working.

"What's all that stuff in the back seat?" asked Shelley, as Adrienne backed the car into the street.

"A bucket and some jars. And my boots. We have to get water samples. I want more than one."

"In a bucket?" Shelley wrinkled her nose.

"Maybe I'll catch a snake or a turtle."

"A snake? Uck. Don't ask me to help you."

"Don't worry. You can help Brad."

"For someone who doesn't like to be teased, you do your share," said Shelley.

"Who? Me? I wasn't teasing. I only said—"

"I know what you said. And I saw the smirk on your face when you said it. Brad isn't a bad guy at all. Believe me."

"I'm trying."

"He isn't."

"I didn't say anything."

Shelley sighed.

Adrienne wondered if Shelley would start dating Brad Ferris. He wasn't her type at all—too moody and too bossy. But sometimes Shelley was like that, too. Maybe they would hit it off after all.

Brad was already waiting outside the lab when they got to school. He smiled when he saw Shelley.

"Did you bring containers for the water samples?" asked Adrienne. "I have several in the car."

"I have some in my car, too."

"Your car? Why didn't you say you had a car? I had to beg my mom to use hers."

"You never asked me. You said you'd drive, so I didn't contradict your orders."

"Orders! I didn't give any orders."

"You did sort of sound as if that's the way it had to be." Shelley sided with Brad.

"Brad can drive tomorrow. And that's an order," said Adrienne. "Do you need anything from the lab?"

Brad shook his head. "Do you?"

"No. Let's go."

"Adrienne, what about Tuck?" asked Shelley.

"He isn't here. We can't wait around. He isn't even enrolled in the class." She turned and headed for the stairs. Shelley and Brad followed.

Halfway across the parking lot, Adrienne saw Tuck leaning against the front of her car, waiting.

"Let's go," he called. "We have work to do, creepy-crawlies to collect."

"How did you know this was my car?" Adrienne demanded.

Tuck smiled and put his hand on her shoulder. "See the old clunker parked over there?" He pointed across the way to a beat up Pontiac. "That's my car. I was sitting in my car when you pulled into the lot. Since you were driving, I assumed this was your car. Old Tucker here isn't always a dumbbell."

She pulled away from him and opened her car door. "Brad, get your containers. We'll put them all in the trunk."

"You're going to make canned creepy-crawlies?" asked Tuck.

"Tuck, this is a serious class," said Adrienne. "Quit making smart remarks every two minutes."

"Whew, don't mess with Adrienne this morning. She's as bad as Brad," he said with a grin.

"Tucker..." She frowned. Was she sounding the way Brad had yesterday? Maybe she was, but she didn't know why. Probably because of Shelley's teasing. Now she felt self-conscious with Tuck around, and she didn't like feeling that way.

"Brad and I will ride in back," said Shelley. "Tuck, you ride up front with Adrienne."

"Are you sure she won't bite me or bottle me?" he asked.

Despite her determination to stay serious, Adrienne felt herself smile. The picture of Tucker Michaels peering out of a glass jar was too funny.

Tuck smiled back at her and ran around the car to get in.

Indian Vale was about a half hour's drive from Pendleton High. The marsh was a low stretch of land, unbuildable because it was so wet. Civilization had crept to its edges but left those few wild acres of wilderness in the center of the suburbs. The lowest section of Indian Vale was called the swamp. A variety of wildlife inhabited this Eastern marshland. The visible creatures included snakes, birds, frogs, turtles, and a myriad of insects. The invisible ones included the minute protozoa and other organisms and creatures inhabiting the dank ground and swamp water. Reeds, grasses, and cattails grew in abundance along with the less prolific and delicately beautiful wildflowers. There was a lot of swamp life at Indian Vale, a lot to be discovered.

Adrienne parked the car off the edge of the road that led into Indian Vale Marsh. The air was still. The sun had grown warmer, so Adrienne and the others left their jackets in the car. They pulled on their boots.

"I'll carry those." Tuck took the bucket filled with jars from her as they started along the dirt road that led to the marsh.

"You don't have to. I'm perfectly capable of carrying my own bucket," she said.

"I know how capable you are. I'll still carry the bucket."

She didn't want a scene, so she let him have his way and carried only her notebook and a couple of pencils.

The four made their way through the soft mud. The swamp around them was alive with sound: birds called above, insects hummed at their feet. A nearby bullfrog croaked and was answered. The only sign of civilization was the litter, probably left by couples who had used the road for a lovers' lane.

The end of the road came abruptly. From there, two narrow overgrown trails branched off.

"We should stick together," said Tuck. "Kids get lost in here all the time. Mr. G. wouldn't love to hear that his elite Pendleton High bio class had to be rescued on their first field trip."

Brad glared at Tuck. Before he could say anything, Adrienne spoke. "Brad, let's all go in together today. Once we feel as if we know the way the paths run, we can separate. You decide where we'll start."

"This way." Brad motioned with his head, indicating the patch that entered the marshland to the right.

Surprisingly there were no arguments over this first decision. They marched single file after Brad. Several birds flew up from the nearby undergrowth, calling warnings of the intruders to the others. Shelly jumped and yelled as a snake slithered across their path.

"Get him," shouted Adrienne, but the reptile was too quick and his camouflage coloring helped him become invisible. "Darn!" she said.

"There will be plenty of others," said Tuck. "Just be sure you don't grab a water moccasin or some other poisonous snake. They don't take kindly to handling."

"Don't tell me." Shelley put her hands over her ears.

"Ignorance isn't always bliss," said Brad. Keep your eyes open and watch where you're stepping. Michaels is right. There are poisonous snakes in here, especially near the swamp."

As they went along, Brad and Adrienne clipped leaves and blossoms from those flowers they knew were not endangered. Adrienne shoved a sample of soil into one of her jars and managed with the help of Tuck to capture a dragonfly with a blue head and iridescent wings.

Brad caught a frog, and they both scooped jars of tadpoles from the first pool of water they came to.

The farther they penetrated into the marshland, the denser the growth became, until the sun filtered only an occasional ray through the overhead branches and even the air felt moist.

"I'm hungry," said Shelley.

"We can offer frogs' legs, fried grubs—" Tuck began.

"Ugh! Stop before I'm sick. My appetite is gone," said Shelley.

"We're almost at the big swamp," said Brad. "Let's keep moving."

Again they fell in single file. Walking became more difficult as mud and water oozed over their boot tops. Mosquitoes and gnats buzzed at them.

"This is far enough," said Adrienne when they reached the edge of a large stretch of still, brackish water. Algae grew along the shore. Bubbles rose from some hidden source below the surface. "Let's get samples, then get back to the lab." She uncapped another of her bottles and scooped up a water sample. Then she prepared to take another.

Shelley complained and slapped at bugs.

Brad was also collecting water samples, while Tuck was amusing himself by sinking his feet into the muck and pulling them out to make a sucking sound.

Before Adrienne straightened up from taking a sample, she spied what looked like a quarter-sized green bubble floating in a patch of algae beneath a low hanging branch. She picked up her bucket, the only container she had left, and waded slowly toward the bubble, doing her best not to make waves or even ripples in the water. She hoped she could scoop it up and get back to the lab without it bursting. If she could, she could test for any gas contained inside, maybe some methane or swamp gas.

She pushed the branch back, wedging it in the bush on the bank, then dipped her bucket deep so as not to disturb the bubble. To her surprise, the bubble bobbed, as if it were round like a ball rather than air trapped in a half orb of liquid and floating on top of the water. As she righted the bucket the bubble sank, then rose again to the surface. A ray of sun speared through the overhead trees, striking her find. A glint of blue, just a dot, showed through the shiny green coating. She flushed with excitement. What had she found? Was this just a bubble? Or was this something else?

She looked around. Brad and Shelley were stooped down near a fallen tree. But Tuck was sloshing in her direction.

"What did you get? A turtle? A frog? A snake?" he asked.

Adrienne shook her head. "I don't know what it is," she said.

Tuck looked in the bucket where the bubble-like object floated in the dark water. "It's the blob," he said, making his voice waver in a spooky way. "Hey, Brad, Shelley, look at this."

Adrienne wished he hadn't called the others. This was her discovery. She wanted to find out what it was before telling them. But it was too late. They hurried toward her.

Brad peered into the bucket. "Looks like a bubble to me," he said. "Or maybe a fish nest of some kind."

"A fish nest?" asked Shelley. "I never heard of such a thing."

"Some fish blow bubbles to make nests for their eggs," he said. "Although I didn't know any fish were living in here."

"Maybe it's an outer-space creature." Tuck put his hands to his mouth and made whistling sounds as if a space ship was landing. "It was left here when a UFO landed. Look at all the cans and beer bottles they left behind. Can't trust those aliens to keep a planet clean."

"Be serious," said Shelley, though her eyes opened wide, and she glanced over her shoulder. "It's just a bubble."

"You're probably right," said Adrienne. "It will burst before we get back to the lab. Well, I'm finished. Tuck, Shelley, will you help Brad and me carry our sample jars?"

"I don't know," said Tuck. "You didn't want any help on the way in. You said you were capable."

Adrienne sighed. His eyes were dancing with mischief. He was impossible, incorrigible, and altogether too likable for his own good.

"Oh, all right, swamp lady. I'll help." He reached for the bucket, but she was reluctant to let go. "Don't drop it," she said.

"And burst your precious bubble? I wouldn't dare." Tuck led the way back to the road.

Adrienne insisted that Tuck hold the bucket on the front seat, which he did, though not without a few cracks. She drove cautiously back to Pendleton High, where they carried their specimens and samples to the lab.

"Let's take a look at your blob," said Tuck when she and Brad had lined one end of the counter each with jars and bottles and deposited the live creatures in larger containers.

They gathered around the bucket and looked in.

"Hey, maybe it is a fish nest," said Shelley. "I see a blue spot."

"Where?" asked Brad. "I don't. But it does look thicker than a plain old bubble."

"Touch it," said Tuck.

"Yuck!" Shelley backed away.

"I have to make some notes before I forget," said Brad.

"Me, too," said Adrienne, reaching for her notebook. "Tuck, leave the bubble alone. If you break it after I got it back here and before I can run tests, I'll—I'll drown you."

"What a bunch of sissies," said Tuck. "You have to guess it's not an ordinary bubble or it would have broken by now." He poked a finger into the bucket. No one moved. His sudden intake of breath was heard by all of them.

"What's wrong?" asked Adrienne. "Did you break it?"

She peered into the bucket and was relieved to see the bubble undisturbed. Turning to Tuck, she waited for the grin and the punch line, so typical of Tucker Michaels. But neither was forthcoming. A slight frown creased his forehead.

"It's not a bubble." He looked down at his hand. "It feels like—like Jello."

"Sure," said Brad. "Let me see." He reached into the bucket. One look at Brad's face told Adrienne that Tucker had spoken the truth.

"Let me," said Adrienne. As she lowered her hand into the bucket, the glimpse of blue seemed to wink at her. The bubble felt medium firm, moist but not exactly slimy, yet not rubbery, either. When she pushed down gently, her finger sunk in slightly, but she left no mark and there was no residue except water on her skin. The bubble bobbed in the water.

A mass of thick gelatin was a good description, she thought, and made some notes in her book.

"I'm not going to touch that thing," said Shelley.

"You don't have to," said Tuck. "What do you suppose it is?"

"I still think it might be a fish nest or maybe a mass of amphibian eggs," said Brad.

"Or maybe a giant sperm!" Tuck joked.

"Gross," said Shelley.

"Sperms have tails," said Adrienne.

"The tail could be under the water. Watch out, girls." Tuck teased.

"Sperms aren't green," said Adrienne.

"How come you know so much on the subject?" asked Tuck, grinning. "Maybe this one is."

"Drop it!" demanded Brad.

They turned to stare at him.

"You shouldn't talk like that," he said.

"Like what?" asked Tuck. "You have the wrong idea. I was talking seriously."

"You were talking scary," said Shelley.

Adrienne stared into the bucket. Again she saw a glimpse of blue. It looks like an eyeball, she thought. A green eyeball with a blue center. A shiver passed over her. "What if it *is* alive?" she said half to herself.

When she looked up, the others were staring at her. But no one answered her question.

Chapter Four

I'm not going to write anymore notes today," said Brad, breaking the silence. "Adrienne, let me have the lab key. Mr. Garrison said we should share, and I want to come in early tomorrow morning and start some experiments with this water."

"You won't touch the—" She hesitated. What should she call the green thing?

"The blob," Tuck filled in.

"No. I won't," said Brad, "but I'd like to see what a sample of that thing looks like under a microscope."

"I'll be here tomorrow morning, too," said Adrienne. "We'll see then." She handed the key to Brad, somewhat reluctantly. "I think I'll pour the water and the, uh, blob into an aquarium, then we'll be able to see it better."

"Not a bad idea. Maybe we can see if it's perfectly round." Tuck grinned, but no one picked up on his comment this time.

Adrienne pulled an aquarium out of the cupboard and wiped the inside with a damp rag. She set up the oxygen pump and filter.

"Maybe you shouldn't run the pump and filter," said Shelley. "That thing came from swamp water."

Adrienne frowned. Shelley could be right, especially about the filter. But what about oxygen? Should she add oxygen? Algae grew well in a balanced fish tank with both a filter and oxygen. She decided to compromise. "I'll leave the filter out, but let the oxygen bubble in. That would be best. If this thing is alive, it might eat algae or something else that's in the water."

"You hope that's all it eats," said Tuck.

"Come on, Tuck," said Brad. "We don't know what the thing is, but all that blob nonsense is right out of a B movie. What could something the size of an eyeball hurt, anyway?"

"Don't say I didn't warn you," said Tuck.

"Adrienne, are you almost ready to go?" asked Shelley.

"In a minute, as soon as I empty this bucket into the aquarium."

"Why don't you use the fish net to scoop up the blob?" asked Tuck. "That way you won't injure it."

"Good idea." Adrienne searched through two cupboards and a drawer before she found a dilapi-

dated fish net. With a cup, she ladled some of the
swamp water from the bucket and then poured it into
the aquarium. She found she'd captured a few more
tadpoles and some mosquito larvae along with the
blob. More observations to add to her notes. Carefully she dipped the net into the remaining water and
slid the basket beneath the green blob. What if it was
a bubble after all and burst when she lifted it out?
They'd all laugh then.

But the round blob settled into the net, surprisingly didn't lose its shape, and didn't squirm as a fish
would. She transferred it without mishap into the
aquarium and poured the remaining swamp water
from the bucket.

"No tail," said Tuck.

"It's not a jellyfish, either." Brad sounded disap-
pointed.

Adrienne guessed that he probably thought he
knew what she'd found, but wasn't saying. "Jellyfish are found in salt water," she said.

"There could be swamp water or fresh water jellyfish," said Brad. "You ought to research before
you say there isn't such a thing."

"And you ought to research before you say there
is," said Tuck.

Brad ignored him.

"I'm ready to quit for today." Adrienne resisted
the urge to join the debate. She didn't know what
she'd found and didn't want to guess. "Shelley, do
you want to come to my house for lunch?"

Shelley glanced at Brad. "Not today, thanks, Adie. Brad's going to drive me home, if you don't mind."

"Why should I mind? Call me later, okay?" She picked up her notebook.

Shelley nodded.

"I'll walk downstairs with you." Tuck followed Adrienne to the door.

"Won't you get in trouble for not being in your English class?" she asked when they started toward the first floor.

"Maybe." He shrugged. "But maybe not. Mrs. Stevens is teaching. I told her I'd be there for the tests. She's okay for an old lady."

"You just said, 'Mrs. Stevens, I'm not coming every day but I'll be here for the tests'? And she patted you on the head and said, 'Tucker Michaels, that's perfectly all right.'?"

Tuck grinned. "Well, I might have mentioned something about working."

Adrienne nodded. "That's what I thought. You lied."

"I didn't. I do have a job."

"What? When? Where?"

"Protecting you from the blob. Every day. Here."

"Be serious."

"I am. You don't know what you've got there; and until you put it back in the swamp, you might be in danger."

"Put it back? I'm not going to put it back." Adrienne pushed the door open. The day had grown extremely warm. She smoothed her hair back from her face.

"What are you going to do with it?"

"Keep it. Find out what it is," said Adrienne.

"Keep it? As in meet my pet blob Igor?" Tuck hunched his shoulders and let his arms dangle loosely at his sides.

"You don't know it's a blob. It could be a plant," said Adrienne, ignoring his act.

"Do you believe that?" Tuck straightened up and walked with her to the parking lot.

"I can't make a judgment until I've observed. That's the scientific way."

"I'm glad to hear you feel that way. How about observing me tonight? At the show? I'll pick you up about seven, and we'll get a hamburger before."

"I'm not—"

Tuck took her hand. "Don't judge until you've observed. Remember?"

All her resolves, not to get involved, left her as she looked into his dark brown eyes. He was serious for once. What could it hurt? And her mother would be delighted. "All right," she said.

"All right? All right! See you later." He jogged toward his car.

"But you don't know where I live," she called after him.

"Sure I do—8234 Markham Road, Apartment 402."

"But how—?"

"I looked you up in the book."

"But I'm not in the phone book."

"I looked in the other book—your science notebook. You wrote your name and address in the front." He laughed and opened his car door. "See you later, Adrienne."

Adrienne, she thought. He didn't call her Adie, the way her other friends did. Adrienne. She liked the sound of it.

When she reached home, her mother was waiting to leave for work.

"When you use the car, honey, you have to be back here on time," she said. "I'm going to be late."

"I'm sorry, Mom. I thought I'd be here earlier." She hesitated. Should she tell her mother about the trip to Indian Vale and the discovery? No, she decided. How could she describe what she'd found? Instead she said, "A boy asked me to the show tonight."

Her mother smiled. "Really? What's his name? How did you meet him?"

"His name is Tucker Michaels, and he's been hanging around the biology class."

"Hanging around? Isn't he in the class?"

Adrienne shook her head.

"But he's interested—in you."

"I don't know, Mom. He asked me to the show, that's all."

"That's wonderful. What time will you be going?"

"Seven. We're going out for hamburgers first."

"I'm sorry I won't be here. I have a meeting with Gary before our accountants go over the books, and we have to plan our orders for next month. Maybe the next time...."

Adrienne smiled. "Sure, Mom. Next time." She doubted there'd be a next time, but she didn't want to spoil her mother's excitement.

When her mother had gone, Adrienne fixed herself a peanut butter and honey sandwich and flipped on the television. She watched a soap opera for a few minutes, then turned it off. She kept thinking about the creature she'd found. Why do I think it's an animal? she wondered. Why do we all think that? She had to do some research but she would tell no one the results. She decided to try the library. Maybe she could learn something from a book. Gobbling the last of her sandwich, she picked up her notebook and purse and headed for the door just as the phone rang. She backtracked to answer.

"Hi, it's Shelley. Guess what?"

"What?" Her tone was curt. She was dying to get to the library and find out what she'd discovered at Indian Vale Marsh.

Shelley didn't seem to notice the impatience in her voice. "Brad asked me out. We're going to play miniature golf."

"Tuck asked me out. We're going to the show."

"And you said yes?"

"You said yes to Brad, didn't you?"

"Sure, but Tucker Michaels..."

"Tucker Michaels what? He's all I've heard about from you since yesterday."

"That was only teasing. Actually, now that I've been around him for a day, I'm certain that he's not your type, Adie. What do you have in common? You're always saying you don't go out because you don't have anything in common with the boys who ask you. Now you've said you'd go out with Tuck?''

"I don't understand you, Shelley. I thought you'd be glad." Actually Adrienne had been asking herself the same question. "So what do you and Brad have in common? He's such a grump, how can you have fun?"

"He's not a grump. You know about Jenny. Besides, I didn't really mean to sound as though I didn't like Tuck. I guess I was just surprised."

Adrienne wasn't so sure that she liked Brad. He was too bossy, too critical, and too narrow-minded. She also had a feeling that he was too secretive. While Tuck on the other hand—irreverent, egotistical, and even immature as he seemed—was . . . what was he? . . . fun. Yes, that was it. If nothing else, she'd have a good time with Tucker Michaels. But did she want to date boys only because they were fun? It was all very confusing.

Aloud, she said, "Haven't you ever wondered why Jenny broke up with Brad?"

"Of course not! Why should I? It's none of my business!" Shelley sounded defensive.

"You're right. It's just that Brad sometimes rubs me the wrong way. Do you know what I mean?"

"No, I don't. And since he didn't ask you out, you don't need to worry about it. You have enough on your hands with Tuck. You might find yourself fighting with him all evening—"

"I doubt it. Anyway, I can't worry about that now. I have to think about passing this biology class. I was on the way to the library when you called. I really have to work on my notes."

"Don't let me keep you," Shelley said crossly.

Why had they gotten into such a dumb discussion, Adrienne asked herself as she dropped the receiver back onto the phone. Grabbing her books, she ran out the door to catch the bus to the library.

The few books at the library on aquatic swamp life told her what she and the others had discussed: the blob could be fish eggs or frog eggs; and she came across descriptions of hydra and protozoa including the amoeba. But these last were microscopic life forms. Unless... Was it possible that for some reason one of the tiny simple organisms had become enlarged, had grown millions of times its normal size? But how? Why? Adrienne snapped the book shut and shook her head. That's too much like the blob, she thought.

After leaving the library, instead of going home, she headed back to school. It wasn't until she was halfway across campus that Adrienne realized she couldn't get into the biology lab. She'd given the key to Brad. Still, she couldn't resist the urge and ran up the stairs to peer through the tiny window on the classroom door. She could get only a glimpse of the aquarium on the far counter near the windows. Nothing seemed changed.

Her footsteps echoed as she went back down the stairs.

"I'm locking up, miss," called Mr. Foley, the janitor.

She waved and went out the door. I suppose I could call Mr. Garrison, she thought as she walked to the bus stop. The problem was that if she'd really found something unique, she knew that he probably would claim it and either give it to the university or to a laboratory to dissect.

She shivered. That would hardly be fair. The thing hadn't hurt anyone. It had been floating quietly in the swamp until she'd interfered. "I have five weeks," she mumbled to herself. "I'm going to make up my own mind. The decision is mine—not Mr. Garrison's, not Brad's, not Tuck's, not Shelley's." She was still talking to herself as she boarded the bus and sat in the first vacant seat. "I'll tell them all tomorrow," she muttered, "all except Mr. Garrison. He doesn't need to find out about it until—"

"I beg your pardon, did you say something to me?" asked the woman who sat beside her.

Adrienne smiled, embarrassed. "No. I was just thinking out loud."

The woman smiled and went back to her book.

Adrienne returned to her uneasy thoughts.

The bus reached her stop, and Adrienne got off. She had made up her mind. Hurrying inside the building, she rode the elevator to the fourth floor.

Chapter Five

Adrienne asked herself a dozen times why she'd said yes to Tucker Michaels. The last time she'd had a case of nerves like this was when she started junior high school. That had seemed like such a big move going from elementary school to the junior high. She'd been sure she'd get lost in the larger school. "And I did get lost," she told her mirror reflection, "and I survived." And she'd survived ever since. "And I will tonight," she said; but she still felt nervous.

When the doorbell rang, the sound startled her so much, she dropped her hair brush on the floor. "Calm, Adrienne," she said. "Calm, calm, calm." She picked up the brush, tossed it on her bed, and went to answer the next ring.

Tuck whistled appreciatively when she opened the door.

"Shhh," she said. "Come in here, before you have all the neighbors looking out to see what's going on."

He grinned his Tucker Michaels grin and stepped inside the apartment. "I don't care if your neighbors know I'm taking out the most beautiful girl in the building."

"Sure."

"Hey, Adrienne, I mean it. Don't you look in the mirror? You're a good-looking chick."

"I am not a hen," said Adrienne.

"Do you take everything so seriously? Chick, dame, fox, girl. Mrs. Stevens would be proud that I know my cinnamons. I meant it as a compliment."

Adrienne tried not to smile. She shook her head. She saw Tuck look around. "My mom is working. She said to tell you she was sorry she couldn't meet you."

"Me, too," said Tuck. "Are you ready? I'm starved."

"Where are we going?" Adrienne picked up her white jacket and her purse.

"To my house," said Tuck.

"Where?" Adrienne wasn't sure she'd heard right. What exactly did Tucker Michaels have in mind, anyway?

"I'm taking you to my house for dinner. Hamburgers, like I promised. My dad is barbecuing outside, and Mom suggested that I bring you. I figured you'd like to know more about me anyway."

"Do you take all your dates home?" she asked.

"I don't date that much." Tuck stepped out in the hall and waited for her. "And I almost never take my dates home. But you were invited."

Adrienne wondered why. She followed him out the door, more nervous than ever. It was one thing to go out on her first date, but another to be taken to the boy's house. She hardly knew Tuck. What would she say to his parents? And why was he taking her there? Most boys never introduced their dates to their parents unless they were serious. Oh, no! she thought. She hoped that wasn't the reason. Tucker Michaels wouldn't know how to be serious. The word wasn't even part of his vocabulary. She pushed the thought out of her head. That was silly. He didn't know her any better than she knew him. He was probably joking, as usual.

But Adrienne realized that Tuck wasn't joking when he turned the car onto Glengarry Street and stopped in front of a neat brick ranch house. The smell of meat cooking over a charcoal fire filled the air.

"You're not nervous, are you?" Tuck asked, as he opened his door.

Adrienne nodded.

He slid back onto the seat and turned to face her. "You don't have to be. There are my mom and dad, who are nice people like me, and my sister and three brothers. Tad might surprise you, though." He was out of the car and coming around to her door before she could ask who Tad was. She tried to ask as they started up the walk, but the front door shot open and four kids raced out onto the porch then down the walk. In a minute, Tuck and Adrienne were circled by three of them. The fourth had stopped and waited near the step. He stared.

"Back off," shouted Tuck, reaching over to take Adrienne's hand. "I'll introduce you, but you have to let Adrienne breathe and move."

But Adrienne was barely aware of the circling children. She was aware of the firmness with which Tuck clasped her hand in his. And she was looking back at the child who waited, four fingers jammed in his mouth, thin hair hanging in his unusual eyes. She knew from his fishlike face that he was retarded. She'd never met anyone who was retarded before.

A plump woman with unruly brown curls appeared in the doorway. "Children, remember your manners," she called. "Tucker, bring your friend in and introduce her."

As they neared the waiting child, he latched himself onto Tucker's arm and clung there. He continued to stare at Adrienne, until she had to look away.

The others jumped around behind them, following them through the doorway.

"I'm Mrs. Michaels." The woman extended her hand. Her handshake was firm and friendly. Her smile and her eyes reminded Adrienne of Tuck.

"Mom, this is Adrienne MacKenzie." Tuck pried his brother loose from his arm.

"This is Tad." Mrs. Michaels put an arm around the little boy. "He's shy at first, but when he gets to know you he's very affectionate." The other children lined up in front of their mother. "This is

Beth," she said, putting a hand on the little girl's shoulder.

"I'm eight and I'm going to camp tomorrow," said Beth.

Adrienne smiled. She remembered how important she'd felt the first time she had gone to camp.

"And these two jumping jacks are Davy and Tom."

"We're six," they said.

"They're twins, but not identical," Mrs. Michaels explained.

"I'm pleased to meet all of you," said Adrienne.

"Is Dad home yet?" Tuck still held her hand, and she didn't want him to let go.

"He's cooking the dinner," said his mother. "Let's go outside. Beth, is the picnic table set?"

"Yes, mother," said Beth. "I'll take Tad out for you." Beth reached for his hand. "Come on," she said. "We're going to eat, Tad. Let's go see Daddy."

Fingers still firmly stuck in his mouth, he let his sister lead him away.

"Tad's five," said Tuck. "He doesn't talk much yet. Mom didn't think there'd be any more kids after I was born. Surprise!"

Adrienne felt her face burn. She'd been wondering why Tuck was so much older. Had he read her mind?

"Make that plural," said Mrs. Michaels, who followed behind them. "I wouldn't trade any of them," she added, walking with them toward the kitchen.

"Not even Tad?" asked Tuck.

Adrienne was startled; that seemed such a personal question to ask in front of her.

Mrs. Michaels didn't seem to mind. She put her hand on Tuck's arm. "Not even Tad," she said. "You two go out into the yard, too. I'll be right there with the hamburger buns."

Passing through the house, Adrienne had noticed that the overstuffed furniture was worn. Toys tumbled from a toy box in one corner of the living room. In the bright-yellow kitchen the dishwasher was already chugging with a load of dirty dishes. "May I help with something?" she asked.

"No, thank you, dear. You're our guest. It isn't often that Tucker is willing to bring a friend home. We're glad you came."

A friend, thought Adrienne. She looked at Tuck but couldn't read the thoughts behind his dark eyes. He hardly knew her. Why had he invited her?

"Dinner's ready!" Mr. Michaels was standing near a round barbecue grill with an apron wrapped around his waist and a spatula in his hand.

"Dad, this is Adrienne MacKenzie," said Tuck as they approached. "Adrienne, my dad."

"How do you do, Mr. Michaels," said Adrienne.

Mr. Michaels smiled. "I do just fine, thanks. I hope you're hungry. I've cooked up a batch of my famous burgers."

"Yes, I am," she said.

"Here are the buns, dear, and the platter," said Mrs. Michaels, coming out the door behind them. "Tucker, you and Adrienne sit on the end of the bench. Beth can sit next to you. I'll take the twins and Tad on my side."

"And I'll sit in the lounge," said Mr. Michaels.

"Am I taking your seat?" asked Adrienne.

"Not at all," Mr. Michaels said with a smile very much like Tuck's. He exuded the same air of self confidence that, up to this evening, Adrienne had always associated with Tuck.

"Come on," said Tuck. He led the way to the table, where Beth was sitting with Tad, who had a spoon stuck in his mouth. Saliva was dripping down his chin.

"Davy, Tom, come to the table," called Mrs. Michaels. The two, who had been hanging upside down from trapezes on the swing set in the corner of the yard, let out a whoop and raced to the table. "Quietly," said their mother. "Are your hands clean?" She inspected them before sending both boys inside to wash.

When the food had been served, Mr. Michaels led the conversation from his place on the redwood lounge. "Davy and Tom, how was your day?" he asked.

The boys took turns telling what they'd done since breakfast, while everyone listened. When they'd finished with their adventures, it was Beth's turn. Then Mr. Michaels came to Tuck.

"And did you take care of your English assignments?" he asked.

Tuck nodded. "Mrs. Stevens said as long as I turn them in, I don't have to be there."

"Be sure you do, dear." His mother smiled at Adrienne. "I've never known Tuck to talk so much about a class as he does about biology," she said. "It's too bad he can't get credit for all this enthusiasm."

Adrienne hoped that he hadn't mentioned the blob. The fewer people who knew about it, the better. "I have another friend who's also sitting in on the class," she said.

"I know," said Mr. Michaels. "Tuck told us. And the other boy is Brad. Frankly, I think this independent study business is a good idea. If the administration gave the students more responsibility, they might get a shock. Even Tucker might buckle down and do some work." To Adrienne's surprise, Mr. Michaels's tone was more affectionate than judgmental. She was also surprised that Mr. Michaels appeared to know so much about Tuck's life. Obviously this was a family that communicated well. She helped herself to another hamburger and let the conversation flow easily around her.

The meal was delicious. Besides hamburgers, Mrs. Michaels had made a big tossed salad and home-fried potatoes. A pitcher of milk made the rounds. Everyone ate with enthusiasm, ignoring Tad's awkward movements as he mashed the food into his face, staring all the while round-eyed at Adrienne.

"Mom, Dad, excuse us, we have to leave for the show." Tucker grabbed a handful of cherries from the center of the table as he got up.

Adrienne blotted her mouth, folded her napkin, then followed him. "Thank you for the dinner, Mr.

and Mrs. Michaels," she said. "It was nice meeting all of you."

"It was nice meeting you, too, Adrienne. Please come again sometime," said Mrs. Michaels.

"Bye," said Davy, Tom and Beth.

Tad jumped up from the bench and ran to Adrienne. He tackled her legs in a surprisingly strong hug. Tuck caught her as she lost her balance.

"Mom," he said.

"Tad, come here," said Mrs. Michaels.

Adrienne put her hand on the little boy's hair.

He tipped his head back and looked up at her. Then he smiled. It was a warm Michaels' smile which made her smile back.

"Tuck and I have to go, Tad." She gently unwrapped his arms as she'd seen his mother do earlier. "I'm glad to know you, too."

He nodded, then ran back to climb on the bench and resume eating.

"Let's go," said Tuck.

Adrienne reached for a napkin to wipe a spot of food from her jeans, a souvenir from Tad's hug.

She and Tuck walked around the side of the house and through the gate.

She waited until they were in the car, then turned to look at Tuck. "Why did you bring me here?"

"So you'd know," he said.

"Know what?"

"Tad," he said. "You saw what he's like. He's a retard, and he'll probably act just the way he did tonight even when he's fifteen or sixty years old. Now you can ask me to take you home." Tuck started the car.

"But he's your brother. And I thought we were going to the show."

"Don't I know that? I'm reminded of it all the time. Actually, you did pretty well. You're only the second girl I've brought here. The last one didn't stay more than five minutes after she saw him. She made an excuse that she forgot she told her mother she'd do something. And a few of the guys will put up with him, but not most."

Adrienne put a hand on his arm. "Tuck, you can't use Tad as a test. Most people have never even met a retarded person. It's a shock. That's not fair."

"Oh, yeah? Tell me about fair, Adrienne."

"Fair is letting me decide whether or not I like you for you, not for your brother or your family. Was Tad the real reason you brought me here?"

"Yeah. Tad." His eyes were dark and full of hurt. This wasn't the Tucker Michaels who kidded and wise-cracked at school. When they reached a red signal, Tuck turned to her. "I guess I blew it," he said. "I should have known that if you liked a blob, you'd like Tad." The laugh that followed had no humor in it.

Adrienne gasped. "You shouldn't talk about your brother like that. He can't help what he is."

Tuck smiled. "I thought you were going to tell me I shouldn't talk about the blob like that."

"Tucker Michaels!"

"Cool off," he said. "I guess I've pushed you far enough. Sorry, Adrienne."

"You should be."

"So what did you decide?"

"About what?"

"About me? Do you like me?" He was the old Tuck again.

"I don't know yet."

"Well, I know about you. I like you, Adrienne. I like you a lot."

Adrienne was stunned. Tuck had made her angry, sad and happy all in the space of a few minutes. She didn't know how to respond to such conflicting emotions. "What show are we going to?" she asked to avoid answering Tuck's question.

"How about a science fiction movie about this green thing that this girl finds in a swamp and..."

She punched him in the arm.

"Ouch! And I didn't even make a move on you," he said. "But if you're going to hit me..." He took her hand.

"Drive," she said.

He laughed and put his hand back on the steering wheel. "If you don't like that movie, how about a romantic comedy? There's a good one playing at the Groveland Theater."

Chapter Six

Adrienne was singing in the shower. Even though Tuck had made no further reference to his feelings about her, she could tell that he really liked her and they had had a very pleasant evening. It was true there had been no passionate kiss at the end, merely a little peck on the cheek and a casual wave of the hand with "See you tomorrow in class," but she felt they were off to a good start. She improvised a chorus on a high note as she threw open the shower curtain and jumped out of the tub.

"Well, someone must have had a good time last night," her mother commented as a broadly smiling Adrienne waltzed into the kitchen.

"Great, Mom," Adrienne said as she sat at the kitchen table and poured herself a glass of juice from the crystal pitcher.

"Where did you go?"

"We had a backyard barbecue at Tuck's house with his family, then we went to the Groveland for a movie. Why are you up so early?" Adrienne reached for the cereal box and filled her bowl.

"I wanted to hear about your date; and with my schedule this week, we haven't seen much of each other except at breakfast."

"Well, you heard. Did you get the raise?"

"Gary said he'd think about it, but I'm pretty sure I will. Are you sure that's all there is to tell about your date?"

Adrienne felt her face grow warm. "Mom."

Her mother put her coffee on the table. "Sorry. I should know better than to get so personal, but I remember all the fun I had in high school. You're a senior this year and no dates yet. I worry that you're missing out on a lot of fun."

"Mom."

"I know. I promised not to nag you. I'm glad you went out, though. Maybe now—" Her mother caught herself. She took a sip of coffee.

Adrienne shook her head. Her mind was on Tuck and on the day ahead. She was eager to get to the lab for four reasons that morning. She wanted to see Tuck, but she also wanted to see the blob. She needed to get there early before Brad had time to do anything to her discovery. She still didn't trust Brad.

Then there was Shelley. Their last words had been too sharp. They had to talk.

She finished her cereal and rinsed her bowl. "I'll wash the dishes when I come home. I have a lot to do at school, Mom."

"Such as meet the boy who took you to the show last night?"

"You never give up, do you Mom? Yes, I'll see Tuck. But I have class and a lot of work to do, too."

"Did he ask you out again?" her mother called after her.

"Not yet."

"Well, flirt a little."

"Mom."

"All right. I'll quit. If we didn't look so much alike, I'd think you weren't my daughter. You aren't like your father, either. He flirted too much."

Yes, thought Adrienne. And now you're divorced. She had to do things her own way at her own speed. She had to be herself. In a way she was almost sorry she'd told her mother about Tuck. She'd never hear the end of it, she knew. There would be questions every day until he'd asked her out again. And maybe he wouldn't want to. Maybe she hadn't passed his test. Maybe that was why he hadn't kissed her goodnight.

Determined not to dwell on that, she grabbed her purse and notebook.

"Are you working both shifts today?" she asked her mother, before opening the door to leave.

"Just tonight. But I have errands to run and shopping to do. Take your key. But tomorrow I have off. If you'd like to invite Tuck over for lunch..."

"I'll see, Mom."

"I'll try not to embarrass you."

"I said I'd see." Adrienne heard the testiness in her voice. She blew her mother a kiss and left the apartment.

Adrienne ran to catch the bus. If she was lucky, she'd get to school at the same time or even before Brad. She guessed that Shelley would probably be with him.

She opened her notebook and reviewed her notes from the previous day. There were observations made of the marsh itself, the collecting of water and soil samples, notes on the leaves and flowers gathered, and last of all the description of the green blob she'd found.

Would her unidentified discovery still be there? What was it? Was it alive? She still had a lot of work to do: tests to run, diagrams to draw, more notes to write. Maybe today would provide some answers.

Adrienne jumped off the bus and ran across the school grounds. She hurried up the stairs. When she reached the lab, she didn't try the door, but peered through the small window.

"Darn," she muttered under breath. Brad and Shelley were already there. Shelley was sitting on a stool watching Brad. It looked as if he was pouring dirt onto a balance or scale.

Adrienne breathed a sigh of relief. At least he wasn't slicing up her blob, something she wouldn't put past him.

An arm went around her waist and she jumped.

"Spying?" He spoke close to her ear.

"No. Yes. Tuck, you scared me half to death," said Adrienne. "I just wanted to see what Brad was doing."

"Is he working on the blob?"

"No. He's weighing dirt."

"Sounds interesting." His voice was sarcastic. "This is the class you love, isn't it? Your mother seems to think so."

"It's not the class," he said. "I thought you'd figured that out by now." His breath was warm on her neck as he leaned close to her.

A shiver ran down her spine. "We'd better go in. I have a lot to do."

"Mm-hm. I know." He opened the door, and they entered the lab.

"Hi." Adrienne headed right for the aquarium before anyone had a chance to reply to her greeting.

"We didn't touch your precious discovery," said Brad.

"I don't even want to look at it," added Shelley.

"Didn't you look, either, Brad?" Adrienne's voice sounded strange even to her.

"No. I have my own work to do." But even as he spoke, he was right behind Shelley, coming to see what had happened to the green object found the previous day.

Adrienne couldn't believe they hadn't looked. Yet the minute she gazed into the aquarium, she knew they'd told the truth.

"Ohmygosh!" said Tuck, voicing her own immediate reaction to what she saw. "I was right!"

"We have to call Mr. Garrison and tell him about this," said Shelley.

"No!" Adrienne glared at her friend. "Don't tell anyone." She turned to face them. "It has to be kept a secret."

"Adrienne, do your experiments with it today. We have to put it back in the swamp," said Tuck.

"No, Tuck. I have to observe it. I need more than a day."

"Then what are you going to do with it?" asked Brad.

"I'll decide that later."

"I think we should dissect it," Brad said.

"You mean kill it?" asked Adrienne. "No way. It's alive. We know that now."

"Do we ever," said Tuck.

They all turned to stare into the aquarium.

"So it grew a little," said Adrienne. "What's the big deal? I was afraid it would die."

"You might wish it had," said Tuck.

"Don't start that blob movie bit again." Adrienne gave him a pleading look.

"Adrienne," said Brad, "it didn't grow just a little. It's too bad you didn't weigh and measure the thing yesterday. You'd better do it today. But you can tell from looking, that thing has at least doubled in size. Yesterday, it was the size of an eyeball.

Today it's like a golf ball. What about tomorrow and all the tomorrows after that? I say kill it before it gets out of control."

"That would be murder," said Adrienne.

"What a bunch of garbage! You step on spiders and kill ants every day. You don't feel as if you murdered them. This thing is no different," said Brad. "I'll do it."

Adrienne stared at the round green blob. The blue spot in the middle was larger, too. "This is different," she said. "If you touch it, Brad, you'll be sorry."

"I won't have to kill it. You'll see. Wait until tomorrow. I bet you agree with me then. I have work to do." He went back to the table.

Shelley put her hand on Adrienne's arm. "Adie, I think you should call Mr. Garrison. He'll come right in and know what to do."

"Shelley, it isn't up to Mr. Garrison to decide what to do. I found this. It's mine."

"I still think . . ."

"Shelley, don't." Adrienne stared at her friend until she looked away.

Shelley wandered back to the table by Brad.

Tuck didn't say any more.

Adrienne took out the balance and a ruler. She scooped a partial beaker of water from the aquarium. When they went back to the swamp, she would have to get more water. She wanted to preserve its environment. She weighed the beaker of water and marked down the weight. Then she took the net and carefully scooped the blob from the aquarium into the beaker. Again she weighed, then subtracted the first amount to get the blob's weight. She recorded the information in her notebook. Before returning the blob to the aquarium, she measured across the top to get an approximate diameter. She included this number in her information.

Brad worked at another table. The lab was quiet except for the bubbling of oxygen into the tank, the movements of the two biology students, and Shelley, who shifted now and then on her stool. Tuck had slipped out the door. Adrienne had seen him go, but hadn't called to him. She had work to do. She was glad, in a way, he was gone. He was a distraction to her when she needed to concentrate.

After returning the blob to the aquarium, she set up a microscope. Should she take a scraping off it and look? She guessed that would be the correct scientific procedure. Mr. Garrison would probably mark her off if she didn't. She opened the lab drawer and took out an instrument with a razor-like end.

Adrienne sensed Brad and Shelley watching her as she put the knife into the aquarium, scraped the blade quickly but gently across the top of the blob, then deposited the soft jelly like particles on a glass slide. She hurried to the microscope and put the slide under the light. Carefully she adjusted the lens. She changed magnification. Frowning, she shook her head. No cells.

"Do you mind if I look?" Brad asked.

"No. Go ahead." She stepped away from the table and let Brad press his eye to the microscope.

"Hmm," he said. "That rules out a few possibilities."

"How can it grow but not show cells?" Adrienne asked.

"Not an egg, either," said Brad. "Eggs don't expand."

Adrienne looked again. This was a puzzle. All she saw when she looked through the microscope was what looked like green jello. She'd have to do more research, go back to the library sometime this week. "Shelley, do you want to look?" she asked.

"Uh-uh. That thing gives me the creeps."

Adrienne shrugged. She went back to the aquarium to see if the scraping had caused any reaction. But there didn't seem to be any change in the blob. It still floated quietly on the surface of the swamp water. In the corner of the glass square the oxygen bubbled continuously.

She carried one of the jars of swamp water which hadn't been oxygenated back to the table. She withdrew an eyedropper of water and put it on a clean slide, then placed the slide under the microscope. She made sketches and notes of the organisms she saw. She did this again several times, each time making sketches and notes. Tomorrow she'd do another scraping from the blob.

She used the same bottle of swamp water to conduct a few further experiments before pouring the contents into the aquarium. She wouldn't have to replenish the water supply for a few days if she could use her samples and maybe she could talk Brad out of his, too.

Back at the table, she sat down and completed a few more notes and observations on her morning's work, then started a sketch of the dragonfly.

At the other table, Brad was cleaning up. Adrienne wondered where Tuck was; and she wanted to talk to Shelley, but her friend, for a change, didn't seem to be in a talkative mood.

"Before you leave, Brad, I'd like the key back. I'll be here earlier tomorrow." Adrienne tried to sound nonchalant.

"Sure." Brad reached in his pocket and tossed the key in her direction. "Shelley, are you ready to leave?"

"Shelley, I hoped we'd have time to talk," said Adrienne.

"Call me later," said Shelley. "Brad and I are going over to the mall."

"Oh. All right. When will you be home?"

"I don't know. Leave a message with Mom if I'm not there."

Adrienne sighed. It seemed as if Shelley was still angry with her. Well, she couldn't help that. She still didn't especially like Brad; in fact, after his suggestion that they dissect the blob, she liked him even less. She put the lab key in her purse. She was glad she'd gotten the key back. She'd try to get there early every day. She didn't like the idea of Brad being there ahead of her and alone with the blob. No telling what he might do.

When Brad and Shelley had gone, Adrienne returned to the aquarium. She stooped down so she could peer straight across at the blob. Was it her imagination, or did the blue thing move? She continued to stare, but didn't see it again. Finally she blinked. "Must have been my imagination," she muttered.

"Are you still here?" Tuck was lounging in the doorway as he had on that first day of classes. "Were you waiting for me?"

"What if I said I was?" she asked.

"I'd say you were probably lying, but I'd be glad." He came to join her near the aquarium. "I still think we should put that thing in the bucket and get it back to the swamp fast. It's out of its natural environment—like that big word?"

"But it isn't," insisted Adrienne. "It's in the swamp water."

"Come on. This lab isn't anything like Indian Vale Marsh, and you know it, Adrienne."

"I don't agree. It might even die if we took it back now," said Adrienne.

"And you don't want it to die. Poor ugly thing, whatever it is." He looked at the blob.

"You don't want it to die, do you?" asked Adrienne.

"I don't want anything to die, Adrienne." Tuck put his arm around her. "But sometimes it might be the best thing. Did you ever think of that?"

Adrienne shook her head. "No." She tried not to think about what she'd do if the blob continued to grow and got too big for the aquarium. She didn't want to pass on the decision-making to someone else the way Shelley did. The blob hadn't hurt anyone or anything. She didn't want to kill it or let it die. She still wanted to keep it here and study it.

Tuck sighed. He turned to face her and his lips brushed hers lightly before he moved away toward the windows. He jammed his hands in his pockets. "Are you hungry?" he asked.

It took a minute before her heart stopped pounding and she could speak in a normal tone of voice. "Starved. Where shall we go?"

"How about your place?"

Adrienne hesitated. Her mother had said she'd be shopping this afternoon.

"How about my place tomorrow and Fat and Juicy's today?"

"You don't trust me?"

"Shouldn't I?" she countered as she busied herself cleaning up the microscope and other instruments she'd been working with. He was always testing, she thought.

"I asked you first." He came to help her.

"It's not that," she said. "My mother said she'd like you to come tomorrow because she'll be home all day and she wants to meet you."

"And today?"

"Today she'll be in and out. Don't rush me, Tuck."

"I didn't think I was. Let's go. Fat and Juicy's it is. I have enough money for two burgers and one shake."

"Don't be silly. I'll pay for my own lunch and yours, too, if you want."

"Now who's being silly? Pay for yours but not mine. I'll make it up when I have a couple dollars."

"You don't have to. I believe in equality." Adrienne turned off the classroom light and closed the door, checking to be sure it locked.

"Equality, huh? A libber?"

"You might say that. I believe in what's fair."

"A girl who'll pay for her own lunch is living up to her beliefs. That's fair." They went down the stairs side by side.

"Where were you?" she asked.

"Did you miss me?"

"I knew you were gone," she said.

"There you go again, not answering the question I asked."

"That's fair, too. You didn't answer my question, either." She laughed at his expression.

"I went to English class."

"Mrs. Stevens must have been surprised."

"Not really. Today was a quiz. I told you I'd go for the tests. Now your turn."

"For what?"

"To answer my question." He held the door for her, and they walked out into a warm summer day.

"What was it?" she asked.

"Did you miss me? You thought I'd forget, didn't you?"

She smiled. "I missed you and I didn't. You're sometimes a distraction, Tuck."

"That sounds promising." He put his arm around her.

Their strides matched comfortably as they went across the parking lot.

Adrienne thought Tuck was probably right. If Brad had left, she'd never have missed him. She wondered if Shelley would, though. She and her friend would have to talk.

"Why are you frowning?" Tuck opened the car door.

This time Adrienne slid across to sit in the middle close to him.

"I was just thinking."

"Is it that much work?"

"No," she said, "but sometimes it's painful."

He started the car. "I know," he said.

Chapter Seven

Tuck wouldn't come up to the apartment even though she invited him after lunch. He had to be the most complex person she'd ever met. She could never second-guess him.

"I'll see you tomorrow," he said. "Would you like a ride to school?"

"But this is out of your way. You live on the other side of Pendleton."

"I'd like to drive you."

"Then I'd like a ride. Thanks. But I want to go early."

"Is a quarter of eight early enough? I'm not even sure the outside doors are open that soon."

"Let's try going then and see," said Adrienne. Brad wouldn't have a chance then, she thought.

"A quarter of eight it is."

Adrienne leaned over and kissed his cheek, then she slid out of the car. He grinned, honked the car horn, waved and drove away. She watched until he turned the corner, then ran up the walk.

Her mother wasn't home yet. She dropped her notebook on the table, then went to the phone and dialed Shelley's number.

"Hi. Who's this?"

"This is Adrienne. Who's this?"

"You mean Adie?"

"Yes, Adie. Who's this?" She guessed either Rory or Toby.

"This is Toby Warner. Do you want to talk to Shelley?"

"Yes, I do."

"Adrienne?" Mrs. Warner came on the line.

"Yes. Is Shelley home?"

"No, I'm sorry she isn't. May I take a message?"

"Just tell her I called."

"I'll do that. She went somewhere with that new boy. I'm glad she found someone to take Alan's place. She was so unhappy when they broke up."

Adrienne didn't want to discuss Brad Ferris with Shelley's mother. "Tell her I'll be here all evening, Mrs. Warner."

"I'll tell her, Adie." Mrs. Warner hung up.

Adrienne wondered if Shelley would return her call. They had grown apart since they'd all been at the swamp. Was it the blob that had changed everything? Or was it Brad and Tuck? Adrienne wasn't sure. Maybe it was both.

"Hi, honey. How was school? Did you see Tuck? Is that his name? It's an unusual one, isn't it?" Her mother slid one bag of groceries through the front door with her foot and carried the other.

"Hi, Mom. Fine. Yes. And yes." She took one of the grocery bags and carried it to the kitchen.

"It's warm out there today." Her mother put the other bag on the table and went to the sink to run a glass of water. "Did you have lunch?"

"I went to the mall—with Tuck. Yes, he's coming to lunch tomorrow. No, he didn't ask me out again."

"You're taking all the fun out of being your mother, Adie." Her mother started to unpack the bag on the table, while Adrienne worked on the one she'd carried in.

"Sorry, Mom. Is it fun being a mother?" she asked. "Are there ever times when you wish you weren't? Do you wish you'd never had me?"

"What questions!" Her mother smiled. "It's kind of late to think about that now."

"Mom, I'm serious."

Her mother looked surprised. "Honey, I guess every parent has days when he wonders if life wouldn't be easier without children. But the answer is no. I'm glad I have you; I've always been glad. Are you feeling neglected? I know I'm not here often, but..."

Adrienne put her arms around her mother. "I'm not feeling neglected. I was just wondering about what it's like to have a baby. No, wait. Don't panic and jump to conclusions," she added when she saw the look on her mother's face. "I mean the responsibility."

"The responsibility is something you accept, and it's good that you're thinking about these things before you marry and have children. Being responsible for another life changes a lot in your own life. There's always that other person to consider." Her mother smoothed Adrienne's hair. "I'm a lucky mother to have you," she said. "I realize that more every day."

"I'm lucky too, Mom. I'm glad we can talk."

"Adrienne, since we can talk, I haven't had to say this before, but maybe I should now. Don't get so involved with Tuck that you forget you have your whole life before you."

"I'm a long way from being that involved, Mom," she said. "Don't worry."

"I'll try not to." Her mother went back to putting away groceries. "I bought some chicken. I thought chicken salad and some hot rolls would be nice for lunch. What do you think?"

"That would be fine, Mom." Adrienne spoke absentmindedly. When you take on responsibility for another life a lot changes, her mother had said. How true that was, she thought. Look how much had changed already since she found the blob. And she had no doubt that it was a life of some kind. She just didn't know what yet.

When the groceries had been stored, she went to her room. "Hi, hi," she said to Tweetledum, in hopes that a miracle would take place and he'd talk

back to her. But he simply squawked and hung upside down on his perch.

She checked on Lancelot, refilling his water bottle and noticed that the platy had given birth to another batch of babies, which were darting in and out
among the plants, keeping out of the way of their
larger and sometimes cannibalistic parents. Adrienne wandered back to the living room then out onto
the balcony. She removed Ding from the rabbit
house and stroked his soft dark fur while she gazed
across the city. What would tomorrow bring?

Adrienne panicked when she woke the next morning and glanced at her clock. The one time she should
have set her alarm, she hadn't. "Fifteen minutes to
do everything! I'll never make it." She started with
the animals. "We can't be friends if Shelley won't
cooperate and at least call me back," Adrienne told
them. "Just because I don't like Brad doesn't mean
I don't like her." She headed for the shower, still
talking to herself.

"Did I tell you that Tuck is going to pick me up for
school today?" she asked her mother as they passed
a few minutes later in the hall outside the bathroom.

"This morning? Now? I'm not even dressed."

"Mom, don't worry. We'll be back for lunch."
Adrienne gulped a glass of juice in the kitchen.

"Then tell him I'm still sleeping." The bell rang as
she said this. "I'll meet him later. Adrienne, I wish
you'd told me."

"I thought I had," Adrienne called. She grabbed
her purse and notebook. "Good morning," she said

when she opened the door to Tuck. "My mom isn't awake yet. You can meet her when we come back for lunch."

Tuck yawned. "Neither am I," he said. "If the school isn't open, I'm going to sleep in the car. Wake me when we can go in."

"I'll do that." Adrienne peeked in her purse to be sure she had the lab key.

They learned at school that Mr. Foley, the janitor, and a couple teachers were also early risers. The door was open. Adrienne and Tuck climbed the stairs to the biology lab.

"Wait," Tuck said, as Adrienne slipped the key into the lock.

"What for?"

"Hadn't you better look through the window first?"

"For what? Brad isn't here yet. He couldn't get in if he was. I have the key."

"What if the lab's filled with green slime, oozing over the side of the aquarium, heading for the door, waiting for you?"

"All right. Enough!" Adrienne glared at him. "Just when I think there's hope for you and that you're getting serious..." She pressed her nose to the small square in the door. "The coast is clear. No sign of the enemy. It's safe to enter."

"Make fun. But until you know what that is, I'm not taking any chances." He closed the door after them and grabbed her hand, pulling her toward him. "I don't want anything to happen to you, Adrienne." He kissed her forehead, her nose, then his lips found hers. When their mouths parted, he held her close for a few minutes before pushing her away. "Don't stand around. There's work to be done."

Adrienne was surprised that her legs carried her across the lab to the aquarium. She stared into the swampy water, not really seeing anything for a minute. All her senses were still across the room in Tuck's embrace.

"Well? Anything new?" Tuck came to stand beside her. "Looks the same to me."

"Me, too. I'll know when I've weighed and measured it," she said.

"Do you want me to help you?"

"You can get the scales out while I get a beaker of water." Adrienne's pulse had finally settled down to a normal rate, and her legs felt like her own. "I want to measure it again, too."

She was scooping the blob into the beaker when Brad and Shelley arrived.

"Any change?" Brad came over to watch. "Looks the same. That's a relief."

As Adrienne deposited the blob into the beaker, she again thought she saw the blue center move. But it could have been an optical illusion caused by the light and water. She didn't say anything to the others. They hadn't seen anything, she knew, or someone would have said something.

When she weighed and returned the blob to the aquarium, recording only a minuscule weight gain, she walked over to Shelley. "I called. Didn't you get my message?" she asked.

"Oh, uh, yeah. I didn't have time to call back."

"We should talk."

"How about this afternoon?"

"I can't." Adrienne glanced at Tuck who was watching the blob now.

"Oh. Well, I can't tonight. Maybe tomorrow. Was it important?"

Adrienne shook her head. "I thought it was, but maybe not."

Was Shelley avoiding her? Was it because of Brad?

Adrienne and Brad completed their work for the day. Shelley watched Brad, while Tuck wandered in and out of the lab. He was there when Adrienne started to clean up.

"Brad, if you're finished with any of your water samples, why don't you dump them in the aquarium?" she suggested.

"I'll dump them down the drain. I'm not taking any responsibility for that thing. You know what I think we should do with it. I'd be glad to see it gone the next time I come in here."

"You talk as if it's a threat to you," said Adrienne. "Are you scared of a little old blob?" She couldn't resist the taunt.

"That's dumb," Brad said.

"I'm scared of it," said Shelley. "Sometimes it's sensible to be scared."

"I'm sorry I asked." Adrienne patted the side of the aquarium. "Poor blob. No one loves you but me." She was sure she saw the blue spot move. Quickly she turned away. "Can I lock up?" she asked.

"Yeah. Let's get out of here," said Brad. "Next week we should go to the marsh for more samples and observation."

"Maybe you'll find your own blob," said Tuck.

"Hah! Who'd want one?" asked Brad. He grabbed Shelley's hand and pulled her out of the room.

"Do you think he's jealous because I found this?" asked Adrienne, turning to the tank for one last look. The blue spot didn't move.

"Who knows what his problem is," said Tuck. "If I were you, I'd tell your girlfriend that he's bad news."

"Why?" She recalled that Shelley had said something similar about Tuck when she'd heard that Adrienne was going out with him.

"Do you know Jenny Forester?"

"I know who she is."

"Did you ever see her smile when she was with him? He wants to dominate."

"Shelley is used to getting her own way. She'll find out soon enough. But she doesn't like to make decisions. So maybe they're a good match."

Tuck shook his head. "It's none of my business, and I don't know the guy that well. Just what I've seen and heard. Let's go. I'm ready for lunch."

Adrienne noticed that Tuck was unusually quiet while they were driving. "Don't tell me you're nervous about meeting my mother," she said.

"A little. Shouldn't I be?"

"She's nice like me."

"That sounds familiar." Tuck smiled. "A taste of my own medicine."

"You'd have to meet her sometime."

"I would? Why?"

"Because I'm going to ask you out, and my mother always meets the boys I date."

"*You're* going to ask *me* out?" Tuck grinned.

Adrienne's heart was racing. She nodded. "Uh-huh. I want to take you to the beach this weekend."

"The beach?" Tuck turned the car onto the side street. He put his arm around her. "That's funny. I was going to take you to the beach this weekend, too."

"I don't think it's funny. I think it's wonderful," said Adrienne.

"You're right. It is." He parked the car, then leaned over and kissed her. "Were you going to do that, too?" he asked.

Adrienne knew she was blushing. "At least twice," she said, then kissed him back before getting out of the car.

He put his arm around her. "You know, you are one special girl, Adrienne MacKenzie. And not at all the way I thought you'd be."

"You're not what I thought you'd be, either," she said.

Tuck's face grew serious. "Yeah. I know. My mom says that sometimes my act gets in the way."

"Why do you play the clown?"

"Who can resist a clown?" Tuck made a face.

"Sometimes clowns seem sad," said Adrienne as they stepped into the apartment-house elevator. She punched the button for her floor.

Tuck sighed. "Sometimes they are. But not lately." He squeezed her hand.

The smell of hot bread greeted them when she opened the apartment door. "Mom, we're here," Adrienne called.

Her mother came from the kitchen. She'd put on a brown skirt and flowered blouse. Adrienne thought she looked very pretty.

"Mom, this is Tucker Michaels. Tucker, my mother, Mrs. MacKenzie."

They shook hands. "Lunch smells good," said Tuck.

"I hope it tastes as good. Adrienne, do you two want to wash your hands after working in the lab?" her mother asked.

"Sure, Mom. Come on, Tuck. I'll show you where."

During lunch they were all stiff at first, trying to make polite conversation. Finally, as everyone relaxed, Tuck had both Adrienne and her mother laughing at stories of some of the antics of his twin brothers.

"Tuck's played a few pranks of his own," said Adrienne. "Right?"

She was surprised that he looked embarrassed.

"That was when I was younger," he said, "at least a couple weeks ago."

Mrs. MacKenzie laughed. "You remind me of my brother. He was always putting a dummy in someone's locker or taping the papers to a teacher's desk or worse."

"Uncle Phil?" asked Adrienne.

"Ask your grandmother sometime, although I'm not sure she likes to remember."

"Taping papers," said Tuck. When he realized that he'd said this aloud, he looked sheepish.

Both Adrienne and her mother laughed.

"The lunch was very good. Thank you, Mrs. MacKenzie," said Tuck. He turned to Adrienne. "I have to go. I promised my mom I'd watch the little kids so she could shop this afternoon."

Adrienne walked him to the door. "I'll see you tomorrow?"

"Right. And let's plan on going out to Lake Lydia on Saturday. I'll bring a lunch."

"You? But..."

"Uh-uh. Equality. Remember?"

Adrienne nodded.

"Ride down in the elevator with me," he said.

"Be back in a sec, Mom." Adrienne closed the door after them.

In the elevator, Tuck pulled her into his arms and kissed her. "Couldn't leave without the second one," he said. "You promised two, remember?"

"Who's counting?" she asked just as they reached the main floor.

Chapter Eight

Lake Lydia was on the outskirts of Pendleton in the opposite direction from Indian Vale Marsh.

True to his word, Tuck had brought a lunch packed in a small cooler.

Adrienne watched the scenery turn from city sidewalks to country fields. She hummed softly with the music on the radio.

"No change in the blob yet?" Tuck asked.

"A tiny weight change. That's all. Maybe Monday I'll see a bigger difference." Adrienne thought about Friday in the lab. Shelley had badgered her to call Mr. Garrison and tell him about her discovery. "He'll have to know sometime," she'd said.

"Why?" Adrienne had asked.

"Because you're writing part of your report on it."

Tuck took her hand. "What are you thinking about?"

"Guess."

"Your little green monster."

Adrienne nodded.

"Why don't you want Mr. Garrison to know about it yet?"

"I'm not sure exactly. Except that if he does know what it is and turns it over to other scientists, I'm afraid they'll do what Brad wants—chop it up. And besides I'd like to find out what it is myself, if I can. Tuck, I think it's unique. It doesn't fit any references I've found in books."

"Have you considered that you might never find out what it is?" Tuck eased the car into the right lane for the Lake Lydia turn off. "And Mr. Garrison will be coming back in a month, then he'll be able to do whatever he wants with it. And if it is unique, it probably should be shared with people who are already biologists."

Adrienne sighed. "I know," she said. "Let's talk about something else."

"Like what?"

"Like can you swim?"

"Of course I can. Can't you?" he asked.

"Not very well."

"Then I'll have to teach you."

Tuck paid admission at the gate to the park. He eased the car into a space in the lot. Adrienne carried the blanket and beach towels. Tuck took the picnic basket. They walked across the expanse of green lawn to the water's edge. The main section of the beach was already crowded with families. Children shouted and laughed as they splashed along the lake shore.

"Down there." Tuck led the way along the sand, around moats and castles, to a space where only a few blankets were spread. "Is this all right?" he asked.

"Fine." Adrienne dropped the beach towels. She spread out their blanket, then wriggled out of her jeans and sweat shirt. She knew she looked good in her new green bathing suit. Tuck shed his jeans and shirt to reveal blue and orange Hawaiian print swim trunks. His shoulders, arms, and back were lightly tanned already. "My mother said anyone would be able to find me in these." He modeled his swim trunks, once again a clown.

Adrienne laughed. "Just hope the fish don't think you're a lure."

"Ah, but I am. I might catch a mermaid named Adrienne."

He took her hand. "Let's try out the water."

They waded into the lake, slightly chilly from a heavy winter runoff despite the warm summer sun.

"Do you mind if I swim out to the raft and back?" Tuck asked.

"Go ahead. It will take me a few minutes to get used to the water." Adrienne ducked down. She inhaled sharply as the cold hit her tender skin. Goose bumps popped out all over. She hugged herself.

"Be right back." Tuck swam smoothly without a lot of splashing. Adrienne admired how effortlessly he moved through the water. She always pictured herself looking like a paddle boat. She jumped up and down trying to get warm.

A few minutes later, she spotted Tuck slicing his way back through the water toward her. He surfaced next to her and shook his dark curls, sending water all over, like a shaggy dog. Adrienne splashed him, a mistake she realized too late as a retaliatory water fight broke out.

"Enough, enough!" she cried when she felt as if she were standing under Niagara Falls.

"Just remember that I didn't start it." Tuck came up behind her and put both arms around her. He rested his chin on her shoulder. "Mmm. I found my mermaid."

"Your mermaid is going to be frozen if she doesn't get a towel around her."

A slight breeze had come up. Adrienne's teeth felt as if they would rattle right out of her head.

"You are cold. Come on. I don't want my girl getting pneumonia."

"Your girl?" Adrienne repeated through shivers.

But Tuck didn't hear her. He'd raced ahead out of the water and returned with a towel which he slipped around her shoulders. Then with an arm around her, he led her back to the blanket.

Adrienne drew her knees up under the towel and gradually felt the warmth soak back into her body. She glanced at Tuck who was stretched out on his side watching her.

"Feeling better?" he asked.

Adrienne nodded.

"How about some lunch?"

"What did you bring?"

"Ah. Wait until you hear." Tuck opened the cooler. "Michaels's delicatessen is now serving your choice of: ham and cheese on rye, bologna, egg salad, or peanut butter and jelly sandwiches."

"You made all those sandwiches for the two of us?"

"I get hungry at the lake. Don't you?"

"Not that hungry. I'll have egg salad."

"One egg salad coming up. And to drink, orange or root beer?"

"Orange. What else do you have in there?"

He smiled and closed the cooler.

"Tuck, tell me."

"Not until you eat all your sandwich like a good girl." He grinned at the face she made. "All right. Chocolate cupcakes, the first apricots of the season, and..."

"And what?"

Tuck smiled mysteriously. "You'll see," he said.

Adrienne suspected that he was teasing again. She nibbled the sandwich, thick with filling and a crisp lettuce garnish. "You didn't make this," she said.

"What do you mean?" Tuck sounded indignant. He wiped a bit of mustard from the corner of his mouth.

"Confess. Your mother packed the lunch."

"My mother did not pack the lunch. She made the egg salad, but I made the sandwiches. Nowadays men are not helpless in the kitchen, you know."

"Sorry. You're right."

"Hmph. This time you're forgiven. And to think I spent all that time squeezing the oranges and the root beer berries to make these drinks."

Adrienne laughed. "Tucker Michaels, you are outrageous."

"Is that all?"

"And cute."

"And...?"

"Are you fishing for compliments?"

"Me?"

Adrienne nodded. "All right. And lovable."

"I'll prove that." He leaned over and kissed her.

"Tuck, everyone will see." Adrienne glanced around her. But the other people on the beach seemed interested in their own activities. No one was staring.

"I want everyone to see my girl. And to know that I love her," he added.

"Tuck—"

"Are you saying you won't be my girl?" he asked.

"No. I'm not saying that. It's all happening so fast. You didn't give me time to think."

"This has happened fast for me, too, Adrienne. But you have to believe in your feelings, trust in your instincts. That's what I'm doing. Please don't tell me I'm wrong." His tone changed. "Am I? I'm not the smartest person in the world, and more often than not I open my mouth before my brain is in gear; but I'm not wrong this time. I can't be. Adrienne and Tuck. We sound right together. We are right together."

A shiver ran through her again, but this time it had nothing to do with being cold. "You're not wrong." She leaned over and kissed him.

Tuck moved closer and put his arms around her. She leaned her head on his shoulder. "You won't be sorry you said yes, Adrienne," he said. "I've never told a girl I loved her before. I don't toss those words around."

"Neither do I, Tucker Michaels," she said.

"Then we'll be fine together. Now you'll find out the big secret." He leaned over, lifted the cooler lid and took out a small package, then handed it to Adrienne. "I hope you like it."

"What is it?" Adrienne sat up straight again. She let the towel fall from around her shoulders then tore at the package wrappings. She wasn't one to unfold each corner neatly. When she opened the box, she could only say, "Oh. Oh, it's beautiful."

"Let's see if it fits." Tuck picked up the silver ring with the band of hearts engraved around the sides. He slipped it onto Adrienne's finger. "Perfect." He put his hand under her chin and raised her head so that she was looking at him.

Adrienne bit her lip and swallowed. She took a deep breath.

"Tears?" he asked.

"Only because I'm happy," she said.

"And she thinks *I'm* crazy." He shook his head.

A half laugh, half sob escaped as Adrienne wiped her eyes with her towel. "Crazy about me," she said.

"Right." Tuck pulled her close again and wrapped the towel around the two of them.

Adrienne couldn't remember when she'd been as happy.

Tuck fed her a cupcake, and she smeared his nose with frosting. They laughed and chased up and down the sand.

Later, they went in the water again. Tuck kept his arms around her. "To keep you warm," he said.

"It's working," she informed him.

He kissed her again.

Then it was time to go. Adrienne twisted the ring and polished it on her shirt when she was dressed. She was sure that any minute she'd wake up and have to feed the animals and get ready to go to school. School, she thought. And her little green problem returned to mind. If she turned in the report she was writing, Mr. Garrison would have to know. If . . .

Traffic was slow and bumper to bumper on the way home. "Everyone went out today," said Adrienne. She turned the radio on.

> "Special love, special girl
> Sets my heart in a whirl . . ."

Tuck sang along with the song. He glanced at Adrienne and smiled. "You're thinking about that thing again, aren't you?" he asked.

"Do you read minds, too?" she asked.

"Faces. Yours says a lot. Adrienne, please think about my suggestion. If you take it back to the swamp, it will be in its original environment. Whatever it is, whatever is supposed to happen to it, should happen there."

Adrienne looked down at her hands. "But I've already changed all that," she said. "And I want to know."

"But maybe you aren't meant to know."

"Then why did I find it? Tuck, you think your solution is right. So do Shelley and Brad each think theirs is the only way. But I'm the one who should decide."

"Unless someone decides for you."

"What do you mean?"

"Nothing. I shouldn't have said that."

"You wouldn't take the blob back yourself, would you?"

"I don't know."

"You just said you love me," she said.

"That's why I might have to do it," he answered. "Don't you understand that?"

"Tuck, will you get that monster movie out of your head? Something like that doesn't exist."

Tuck sighed. "All that certainty from a girl who told me not too long ago that what she's found is unique and doesn't fit any reference she's come across. How can you be sure I'm wrong, Adrienne?"

"I don't know, but I am," she answered.

For a while they rode in silence. But both of them were still thinking about the same thing—the blob.

Chapter Nine

Wednesday rolled around again. A week had passed since the trip to Indian Vale Marsh, a week since Adrienne had found the blob. It seemed much longer, so much had happened.

As usual Tuck picked her up for school. "I'll leave a pitcher of orange juice for you two in the refrigerator," said Mrs. MacKenzie as they were leaving.

"Thanks, Mom. Today is going to be hot. We're going out to Indian Vale again," Adrienne said.

"Do you have mosquito repellent?" her mother asked.

"I do. My mom sent a whole can," said Tuck. "See you later?"

"Not me," said Adrienne's mother. "I'm working a double shift today. If you come back here, you kids behave yourselves."

"Don't worry," said Tuck. He winked at Adrienne.

She smiled and blushed.

Except for their disagreements about the fate of the blob, a relationship couldn't be more perfect than hers and Tuck's, she thought. If only she could patch things up with Shelley, life would be terrific.

But Shelley hadn't been delighted with the news that Tuck and Adrienne were going together. Was she jealous? Shelley was still going out with Brad. Both on the rebound. But Adrienne couldn't tell her friend that. They couldn't seem to talk at all anymore. It bothered Adrienne. It didn't seem to bother Shelley at all, Adrienne thought, as she rode beside Tuck toward school.

Tuck was parking his car when Brad drove into the lot and parked beside them.

"Ready to go back to the marsh?" asked Tuck as the four of them met to walk toward school.

"I don't know why you're tagging along," said Brad. "Don't you have some English to do?"

"Not until Friday," said Tuck. "You're going to be honored with my presence. Count yourself among the lucky ones, Ferris." He winked at Shelley, who was frowning.

"I'm surprised you can carry your head upright, Tucker Michaels. It's so swollen with your good opinion of yourself." Shelley said.

"If I don't love me, who will?" Tuck smiled at Adrienne when she squeezed his hand.

"Lighten up, Shelley," said Adrienne. "Can't you tell he's teasing?"

"Doubtful," said Brad. "Let's get our collection jars and get out of here. It's going to be sweltering today. I doubt the marsh is going to be a pleasant place."

They ran up the stairs, their feet making enough noise to be a whole class rather than four students. Adrienne unlocked the door and went across the room to the counter where she'd left her bottles, jars and bucket. She glanced at the aquarium, bubbling softly nearby. "Look!" she shouted, then wished she hadn't as the others crowded around. If she'd kept quiet, maybe no one would have noticed, except her, that the blob had grown again. All week it had been the size of a golf ball. Now it was tennis ball size, sinking slightly lower in the water than before.

"Oh, no!" exclaimed Shelley, "Creepy! Adie, you have to call Mr. Garrison now. I can't stand looking at that thing one more day."

"Then don't," said Adrienne. "You don't have to come to this class, Shelley."

"Who elected you president?" asked Brad. "Shelley can come if she wants to."

"Then she'll have to accept whatever I discover," said Adrienne. "I'm not getting rid of the blob, and I'm not ready to call Mr. Garrison. So it's a little bigger. A tennis ball never ate anyone. If I recall, you said something similar yourself, Brad, right after I found the blob. You told Tuck he was ridiculous to talk about a blob the size of an eyeball hurting anything. We're actually in agreement about something."

"At least I have enough sense to change my mind. Let's get out of here," said Brad. "Shelley and I are driving together. We'll meet you there, if Michaels's car can make it."

"Yeah? That can of bolts you drive, Ferris, is just like you: all flash on the outside with no guts inside."

Brad took a step toward Tuck.

"Let's go, Brad. His big mouth fits in his big head," said Shelley.

"You two sound like kindergarten brats," said Adrienne. "Listen to yourselves."

"The president is speaking again," said Brad. "Let's go." He handed Shelley a couple bottles, then they left the lab.

"It's getting tense with those two." Tuck stooped down to study the blob. "You know, Adrienne, if this thing doubles every week, it won't be long before it will fill up the lab."

"Don't be silly. Everything stops growing eventually. Although, if Brad were here and it got that big…"

"He gets to you, too, huh?"

Adrienne nodded. "I think you ask for it, though."

"I can't help it. The guy thinks he's better than the average boor."

"Boor? Where did you learn that word?"

"That's a Mrs. Stevens speciality. I've heard it once or twice."

"I bet," Adrienne. "Your act, again?"

Tuck smiled and shrugged. "Old habits are hard to break."

"Are you trying?"

"How do you mean that?"

"You know how I meant it." They were both serious now.

"Yeah, I am. I guess everyone has to grow up sometime. Which brings us back to the blob. We could take it back to the marsh today."

Adrienne tried to smile. "No we couldn't, Tucker, dear."

Tuck sighed. "Somehow I knew you'd say that. Grab your bucket and let's go. You don't want Brad to get all the good samples."

"There's more than enough for both of us at Indian Vale. I wonder if there's another blob. Wouldn't it be something if we found two?"

"Not a chance. That thing is unique. Remember?" added Tuck.

"Of course I remember," said Adrienne. "That's why I don't want to give it up or tell Mr. Garrison. This could be one chance in a lifetime. And when those guys get hold of it, we'll get squeezed out, not to mention what they might do with it."

"I suppose," said Tuck. "Still..." He frowned and looked at the aquarium again. "Race you to the car."

"You'd better not. You're carrying two jars and a bottle. I'd like them in one piece when we get to the marsh."

"Adrienne, you never let me have any fun." He made a face.

"Tough," said Adrienne. "Suffer." She kissed Tuck on the cheek.

"Oh, I love suffering like that," he said.

By the time Adrienne and Tuck got to Indian Vale Marsh, Shelley was sitting in Brad's car, but he was gone.

"Is everything okay?" asked Adrienne, poking her head in the car window.

"Sure, if you like mosquitoes trying to carry you off for dinner and creepy-crawlies jumping out at you from every clump of green. I'll stay here, thanks."

"We have some mosquito spray," said Tuck. "You're welcome to use some."

Shelley shook her head. "Uh-uh. And tell Brad to hurry up."

"Tuck, why don't you go ahead?" asked Adrienne. "I want to talk to Shelley for a minute. I'll catch up."

"I promise not to catch a blob without you." Tuck took her bottles and the bucket and hiked ahead. "I'll wait at the end of the road for you," he called.

"I won't be long." Adrienne turned to Shelley. "Mind if we talk for a minute? I've called you a couple times. I guess you didn't get the message."

"I guess you didn't get my message, either." Shelley didn't move to open the car door, so Adrienne took the initiative and slid into the back seat.

"When did you call?"

"Not that message. The one I've been sending. I don't like Tucker Michaels, and I hate that blobby thing you found. Adie, I can't see why you'd want to keep either one."

Adrienne took a deep breath. "We've been friends for a long time, Shelley. I guess it's fair to talk straight. I love Tuck. You don't know him at all. And the blob is important to me. I think I've found something special. I don't want to dump it or kill it. And if I tell Mr. Garrison, he'll come to school and take it over. You know how adults are. Pretty soon you'll believe he discovered it."

"Who cares? The thing gives me the creeps."

"But it doesn't give me the creeps," said Adrienne.

"You only think of yourself," said Shelley.

Adrienne opened her mouth, but no response came out for a minute. "That sounds like Brad," she said.

"You don't like him, do you?"

"No. But I guess that doesn't matter. I think you're on the rebound from Alan. Eventually you'll see what kind of guy Brad really is."

"But you won't see what kind Tuck is. Is that right?"

"I'm not saying Tuck is perfect. I just happen to know that there's more to him than the swaggering clown image he projects. But you don't have to like him any more than I have to like Brad. What about us and our friendship?''

"It's kind of hard to have a friend who prefers a slimy green thing over her friends.'' Shelley folded her arms and slid down in the seat.

"In other words, if I don't do what you want, you don't want to be friends? Can't you try to understand my side?''

"The thing is disgusting and it's growing. What more is there to understand? I think you're sick, Adrienne. I've even thought of calling your mother and telling her about it.''

Adrienne opened the door and got out. "I guess we can't see things the same way anymore, Shelley,'' she said. "I'm sorry.''

She felt like crying as she walked along the road toward the swamp. It didn't seem to bother Shelley to cancel their friendship so easily. Adrienne wondered how much was Brad's influence. Or was she herself being selfish? Was the blob a threat? No, she decided. She took a deep breath and put her shoulders back. Taking longer steps she increased her pace. I have to do what I think is right, she thought. No matter what.

"I'm glad you're here. Did you get things straightened out with Shelley?''

"Not really. Let's take the other path this time. I want samples from the other side of the swamp. Watch for anything different that I didn't get last time.''

"Aye, aye.'' Tuck tramped along the narrow path with Adrienne leading the way.

They gathered some more plant samples, some that she hadn't seen on their last trip. They took more water and dirt. There were no unusual blobs. They almost caught a small turtle, but it was too smart for them and escaped.

Adrienne kept up such a pace that Tuck finally called to her to slow down. He put the bucket and bottles down. "Come here," he said, pulling her into his arms. He smoothed her hair off her sweaty forehead, then kissed her lightly. "You're upset about Shelley, aren't you?"

Adrienne bit her lip to keep back the tears that burned again behind her eyes. "Do you think I'm selfish wanting to keep the blob?" she asked.

"Is that what she said?"

Adrienne nodded.

Tuck sighed. "Not selfish. Maybe idealistic. Each of us has a different idea about that thing. I'm hoping that patience will win you over to my side."

"It probably won't. I'm stubborn, too."

"But I love you. And you love me. So we'll both wait and see what happens. If it doesn't swallow us before Mr. Garrison comes back, then the problem will take care of itself."

"You sound almost as bad as Shelley. But at least you try to understand." Adrienne kissed him, then pulled away. "This is not exactly the most romantic spot in the world. Let's go back to the lab. I don't want Brad to get there before me."

"You have the key. Remember?"

"That's right. Well, I'm finished. Let's go."

"Lead on, pres."

Adrienne stuck her tongue out at him. "Boor," she said.

Surprisingly she and Tuck got back to the lab before Brad and Shelley.

"There were two of us to collect," Tuck reminded her.

Adrienne wished Shelley were there to hear him. Even if he didn't like Brad, Tuck understood the disadvantage he was working under, with Shelley sitting in the car.

She set up the balance, then hunted for a larger beaker. "Time to weigh in, Charlie," she said, leaning over the aquarium. This time she was sure the blue spot, barely visible through the thick gelatinous mass, moved.

Chapter Ten

I won't be staying while you work today," Tuck said as they climbed the stairs. "Mrs. Stevens is giving her halfway test today. Three weeks over already."

"Good luck. Did you study?" Adrienne asked. She fished in her purse for the lab key as they reached the upper landing.

"Of course. Since I met you, I've reformed. Didn't you know?"

"No I didn't know. What did you get on the last test?"

"Seventy-five."

"That's reformed?"

"For me. Besides, it was a hard test, and she marks on a curve. Give me time. I have to learn how to study. I never did much of it before."

"All right. I'll give you two more weeks."

"Thanks a bunch. Listen, I'll meet you here." Tuck left her outside the lab. He whistled as he strolled down the hall.

Adrienne watched him go, then turned to insert the key in the lock. But as she did she glanced through the window and inhaled sharply. "How did he get in there?" she asked furiously. She withdrew the key and opened the door. "Brad, how did you get in without the key?"

Brad continued what he was doing with a beaker of water.

"Brad Ferris, I'm talking to you."

"So what am I supposed to do? Bow? You sound like my mother, Adrienne. Nag, nag, nag."

Adrienne took a breath and tried to calm down. "Mr. Garrison gave me the key, and I'm responsible," she said in a more even voice. "How did you get in? Did Mr. Foley open the door for you?"

"Mister who?"

"Mr. Foley, the janitor."

"I don't even know the janitor. I made a key when you gave me yours. I didn't expect you'd be willing to share the one and only. You're so protective of that thing over there." He waved his hand in the direction of the aquarium. "And I was right. You have to be camping in the parking lot just to get here before me every morning. Right?"

Adrienne went to her work table and put her notebook and purse down. "No, I'm not. But you couldn't blame me if I did. I wouldn't put it past you to kill it."

"You'll be asking me to do just that before long," said Brad, not bothering to face her.

"That would be the day."

"Instead of griping at me, take a look in the aquarium."

"You better not have done anything." Adrienne hurried to the tank.

For a minute there was only the sound of Brad pouring water and the soft clink of the beaker being placed on the balance.

Adrienne exhaled softly. She stooped down so she could get a good look at the blob. In another week it had again doubled in size. The tennis ball was now a baseball. The blue spot inside was definitely larger, too, but not very visible. Yet, where the light was strongest and if her eyes weren't deceiving her, she thought she could make out a curved shape of some kind.

If only I could see better, she thought. I'm going to put a light behind this thing, then maybe I can tell what's inside. But not while Brad is here. She glanced at her fellow student, bent over his work table.

"It looks healthy," she said.

"Healthy. Disgusting. Wait until I tell Shelley." He went to the sink and slowly poured out previous swamp water which could have been added to the aquarium.

"You'll just upset her. Why bother?" Adrienne asked.

"Don't you want her to know?"

"I don't really care; but knowing Shelley, I'd think she'd rather not talk about it."

"I wouldn't be too sure. Where's your obnoxious partner?"

"I don't know whom you mean."

"Sure you do. Tucker Michaels." He spooned some marsh soil onto a small glass dish.

"Tuck had an English exam."

"He'll probably flunk again," said Brad over his shoulder.

"How does it feel to be perfect?" Adrienne checked the oxygen hose to be sure that it was flowing well.

"You ought to know better than I do. After all, Adrienne MacKenzie knows the answers to everything."

"I never said that." She glared at his back, but he didn't turn around.

"You didn't have to. I hope you're ready to be responsible for whatever that thing turns out to be if you don't listen to me. If I were as bad as you seem to think, I'd have killed it then rinsed it down the drain long ago. I may still do that. I'm enrolled in this class, too, you know. And Mr. Garrison *did* say we could work together," he added.

"Don't do it." Adrienne spoke through clenched teeth. Why couldn't he turn around and face her while he talked? Instead he continued working as if she were not worthy of his full attention.

"When it's too big for the aquarium, I will," said Brad. "That's a promise, Adrienne. You aren't the only one who has an opinion on what's right."

"It's not yours to decide on," she said.

Now he turned to face her. "It is when your decision is wrong."

"But it's not wrong. I know it's not."

"Your opinion again." He continued with his work, making notes in his book.

Adrienne went to work, also. Brad and Shelley. They were both against her. What about Tuck? she wondered. What would he say when he saw the size of the blob? She could guess. The same thing he'd been saying. Let's take it back to the swamp. But that's the wrong decision, too, she thought.

While she analyzed, weighed, measured, cataloged, and tested the latest samples collected at Indian Vale, she thought about how much the discovery of the green blob had changed her life. She wanted a chance to study it. She wanted to know what it was. She wanted it to have a chance to exist. She'd touched it. Everyone but Shelley had touched it. And nothing terrible had happened to them. No one's skin had peeled off. No one had broken out with green warts. It hadn't burned or stung or, even caused a rash. There was no evidence that what she'd found was dangerous. Simply because it was growing didn't make it bad.

She had to force herself to go back to her notes and to repeat experiments.

"Well, I'm finished for today. I'm going to pick up Shelley and take her to the beach. See you tomorrow, Adrienne." Brad capped his sample jars and put away his lab equipment.

"I want the key you made," said Adrienne.

A half smile curved up the corner of Brad's mouth. "I'm not your stupid boyfriend," he said. "I might have to get in here sometime when you're not around. Sorry. I'm keeping the key."

"Tuck is not stupid! And Mr. Garrison isn't going to like you making an extra key."

"Mr. Garrison will never know. Will he?"

Adrienne slammed her notebook shut. He knew she wasn't a tattler. What Shelley could possibly see in him she would never know.

Brad strolled out of the lab, humming under his breath.

When she was sure that he had left, and she'd calmed herself enough so she could concentrate, Adrienne began her work with the blob. She weighed and measured. No doubt at all about the growth this time. She hooked up a strong light and held the big beaker in front of it. The beam penetrated most of the gelatinous mass. But in the very center lay a curved shadow, rather irregular in outline. It moved several times, changing shape for a minute, then returning to its curve.

Slowly, Adrienne walked back to the aquarium. The blob barely fit in the fish net. She'd have to bring a strainer from home. "I've got to be very careful with you," she said as she lowered it back into the water. "Very careful."

"Psst."

Adrienne jumped. "Oh, Tuck, you scared me."

"Sorry. Where's everyone?" He sat on the edge of the lab table.

"Only Brad came today, and he's left already. Tuck, he made his own lab key."

"I'm not surprised."

"What if he dissects the blob when I'm not here?"

"Don't worry. We'll try to be here as early as possible every morning. You know Mr. Foley would let him in anyway. He's seen all of us here."

Adrienne sighed. "I suppose you're right. Still, I think that was sneaky."

"That's lovable Ferris." He jumped off the table. "So, how's Charlie doing? Holy shsh!" Tuck looked into the aquarium. "Why didn't you tell me it was this big?"

"Because I know what you're going to say."

"Adrienne, I know I sound like a broken record, but you have to agree with me. You won't have much choice pretty soon. This thing will outgrow the aquarium. Then it will die if you don't put it in something bigger—like the swamp. I'll take you to visit after you put it back. How about it?"

She shook her head.

"Honey." Tuck turned her to face him. He put his hands on her shoulders. "Look at me. It started out in the swamp. That can't be a bad place for it. That's where it was meant to be."

"No. I don't think it's going to grow much more."

"You don't think. But you don't know. You can't know. You don't even know what it is, Adrienne."

"Tuck, the worst that could happen is that it turns out to be some sort of monster, like in the horror movies. Right?"

Tuck nodded.

"If that was going to happen and we returned it to the swamp, it could spread all over and endanger a lot of people. In the school, it would be contained. So you see, we have to keep it here."

"I thought you said I was silly to be thinking B movie blob. That was your term, wasn't it?"

"You are silly. That's only supposing the most ridiculous," she said.

"Ah. But we aren't assuming the most ridiculous, are we? So we could take it back and nothing would happen to any innocent people and whatever it is could grow and live happily ever after."

"No," said Adrienne.

"No what?"

"Just no. We're not taking it anyplace."

"Maybe *you're* not."

"Tuck, don't." She spoke as seriously as he had. "It isn't going to hurt anything or anyone. It's as big as a baseball, that's all."

"Right now. And each week it grows larger."

"Only until it reaches the right size."

"The right size for what? To eat Pendleton?"

Adrienne turned away from him and pretended to be busy cleaning up the lab equipment. Did she dare tell him that she had a guess? That despite the fact she couldn't find any mention anywhere that such a thing existed or could exist, she thought she knew what the blob might be?

"Why are you shaking your head?" Tuck slid onto the stool beside her.

"Let's not argue about this," she said.

"One more week, Adrienne. I won't wait for it to be a beach ball."

Adrienne didn't look at him, and she didn't argue. She also kept her suspicions to herself.

Chapter Eleven

Aren't you going to ask me what I got on the half-way test?'' Tuck opened the school door for her.

They started across the lawn toward the parking lot.

"All right. What?"

"Eighty-seven percent."

"That's not bad. If you keep going you could score a hundred percent on the final in three weeks."

"And the week after that I'll be elected president of Mensa." Tuck shook his head.

"You have to believe in yourself, Tuck. That can help as much as studying sometimes."

He put his arm around her. "I have you to believe in me. That helps more than studying sometimes."

"Did you notice that the blob didn't get any larger?" she asked, changing the subject.

"Of course it didn't. This is only Friday. The blob grows noticeably once a week. Wait until Wednesday."

Adrienne wished she hadn't brought up the subject. She hadn't realized that Tuck was that observant, and the fact that he said noticeably made her wonder if he was aware of the small gains in both shape and size made during the week, culminating in the noticeable change each Wednesday.

"Want to stay for lunch today?" she asked, shifting to a more neutral subject.

"Sure. What are you making?"

"Peanut butter and honey or tuna fish with mayonnaise and lettuce."

"Tuna sounds good. Shall we stop at the store for some canned soda?"

"No. I made some fruit punch before breakfast this morning."

"Then let's head for MacKenzie's Mansion for the finest in sandwich cuisine." Tuck bowed when he opened the car door. "Your car, madame."

"Very good, sir," said Adrienne. "Home, Tucker."

The warm summer breeze blew her hair as they drove toward the apartment. This summer was perfect so far. She liked independent study. And the secret she thought was soon to be revealed by the blob made the class even more exciting. Then there was Tuck. Who'd have dreamed that she'd fall in love this summer, too? And with Tucker Michaels of all people? Not me, she thought. But I'm glad I did. She twisted the ring on her finger, glanced at Tuck and smiled.

"It's so nice out, let's eat on the balcony," Adrienne suggested when they entered the apartment. "Before I fix sandwiches, I'm going to take the animals out for air." She slid the glass door open. Seeing the rail made her remember the times she'd stood there and thought about being alone. Not anymore. Not with Tuck. "Come help me. You can carry Lancelot, and I'll take Tweetledum."

"How do you hold a guinea pig?" asked Tuck as she pointed to the table where the cage was.

"You leave him in his cage, silly." She poked a finger through the wire to pet the small animal. "We're going outside today," she said, then handed the cage to Tuck. Next, she unhooked Tweetledum's cage from the stand in the corner.

"What does he say?" Tuck asked.

"Squawk, screech, chirp," said Adrienne.

"Smart bird, huh."

"Just like his name."

"Oh, yeah." Tuck laughed.

They carried the cages outside. "We'll leave them out for a little while, but I don't want them to get too warm. You sit down and watch them, Tuck. I'll make the lunch."

"Watch them do what? They won't go any-where."

"I know, but it makes me nervous to leave them out there by themselves."

"They aren't by themselves. The rabbits are out here. You leave them here."

"But they have a little house. I don't know. Lancelot and Tweetledum seem more fragile than Ding and Dong. Maybe because they're smaller."

"All right, I'll animal sit." Tuck sat on one of the lounges.

Adrienne patted his head. "Be back in a few min-utes."

"While you're busy, I'm going to teach this bird to say something," he called.

"Good luck. I've only been trying for over a year," she answered.

In the kitchen she opened a can of tuna fish, then made thick sandwiches on whole-wheat bread. From the balcony she could hear Tuck saying, "Hi, bird. Hi, hi. Pretty bird." She put the lunch on a tray and carried it outside. "Have you had any luck?" she asked.

"Sure. Listen. Hi, bird. Hi, hi."

Tweetledum squawked.

"Did you hear him?"

"I heard him squawk," said Adrienne.

"No. He said, Hi, bird. Hi. Except he said it in bird language."

Adrienne laughed. "Oh, I see. Why didn't I figure that out?"

"Takes another bird brain to understand."

Adrienne placed the tray on a small table between the two lounges. "Don't put yourself down like that, Tuck."

"Is that what I'm doing?"

"Mm-hmm. If it's not your act, you're demeaning yourself. You shouldn't do that."

"Someone else will do it for me, you mean?"

"Tuck! That's not what I mean at all. You've got a good brain. Use it."

"Oh, oh. You're starting to speak parentese."

"What's that?"

"The language of all parents. 'You are my son or daughter. Therefore, you are smart. You must get good grades. You may not fail. You must make us proud. This is who you are. Do not be anyone else. It is not allowed.'"

"Tuck, you have nice parents. They seem to love you a lot."

"They do, I guess. But they nag a lot. And my dad has a great 'no son of mine' speech."

"My mom says that's because parents care."

"That doesn't make it any easier to hear, especially if the class you're flunking doesn't make any sense to you even if your father got an A in that subject when he went to school."

"I suppose you're right."

"Your mom doesn't seem to nag you much."

"She does her share, about stupid things, too."

"Such as?" Tuck asked.

"Such as, when are you going to go out with boys? When are you going to date? Why aren't you having more fun in high school?"

"Now there's nothing left for her to nag about, is there?" asked Tuck.

"Sure there is. When are you going to clean your room?"

He laughed. "The universal nag."

They nibbled their sandwiches and relaxed in the lounges.

"Good lunch," said Tuck when they'd finished eating. "Is there any more punch?"

"I'll bring the pitcher."

After pouring another glass of punch for Tuck, Adrienne took the rabbits from the cage. She handed one to him, and she took the other. She stroked the soft brown fur of the one she held.

"You really care about those animals, don't you?" Tuck asked.

"They've kept me from being lonesome a lot of times," said Adrienne.

"There are times when I think it must be great to be an only child."

"Not when your father is gone and your mother is at work," she said. "Not when you have no one to talk to."

"What about Shelley? She's your friend."

"Was my friend. And Shelley isn't always willing to listen," said Adrienne.

"I am," said Tuck.

"I know. Thanks." She relaxed in the lounge. The sun's rays warmed her. A soft breeze blew across the balcony. I could sit like this forever, she thought. When the shadows had changed, Adrienne got up. She slipped her rabbit back into its house then took the one Tuck had been holding. Both rabbits were used to handling and always seemed to enjoy being petted.

"I'll help you take Lancelot and Tweetledum back inside." Tuck stood up and stretched. "Then I have to leave. I have homework."

"So do I." Adrienne handed him the guinea pig cage. "I want to go over my notes from the first three weeks and try to organize them."

When the animals were back inside, Adrienne walked with Tuck toward the door. He stopped and put his arms around her. "You have freckles on your nose," he said.

"I know. And you don't."

"Will you share yours?"

"You can have them all." She rubbed her nose against his, then their lips met, and Adrienne forgot all about freckles and animals and even the blob. She thought only about Tuck. "Mmm," she said as he pulled back.

"Double mmm," said Tuck. He hugged her tight, then turned to leave.

"Do you have to leave?" she asked.

Tuck hesitated. "Yes. I'll see you in the morning."

Adrienne ran to the balcony to watch him. She waved when he looked up at her and blew a kiss.

The phone rang and she ran back inside.

"Hi, honey. Did you have lunch?"

"Yes, mom. Tuck just left."

"I don't want him staying too long."

"I know, Mom. He didn't stay too long." He didn't stay long enough, Adrienne thought.

"Listen, honey. I'm going to stay and work the late shift, too. The part-time girl called in sick. Can you fix yourself some dinner? Maybe you could call Shelley to come over for a while."

"Don't worry about me, Mom. I'll be all right. I have some school work to do."

"All right. I'll see you in the morning."

"By, Mom."

Adrienne wandered to her room and picked up her notes. This was probably a good time to sort them out and organize them. She took an old ring binder from her closet and some loose-leaf paper from a shelf. At first she was going to separate the plant and animal life only. Then she decided to make a separate section on the blob.

It was after five when Adrienne looked at the alarm clock ticking away near her bed. She'd gotten so involved in organizing her biology notes and seeing the changes she'd recorded in the blob that she hadn't realized how much time had passed.

She got up and stretched. Going to the kitchen, she opened the freezer and took out a frozen chicken pie. She set the oven and popped the pie inside. Then she walked to the sliding glass doors and looked out. Dark clouds were forming on the horizon, and she thought she heard a rumble of thunder in the distance.

While she waited for her dinner to cook, Adrienne picked up the phone and called Shelley.

Sam answered.

"This is Adrienne. Is Shelley home?" she asked.

"Nah. She's out someplace with bad Brad," Sam said.

"Oh. Well, tell her I called."

She hung up. Shelley and Brad seem to be getting as serious as Tuck and I, she thought. If only meeting those two boys hadn't interfered with their friendship! Had it been the boys who had interfered? Or was it the blob? Could it be the fact that she had been the one who discovered it and not the blob itself? There were no straight answers to the problems that had started three weeks ago. She wondered if there ever would be.

Rain started while Adrienne was eating dinner. She checked on the rabbits to be sure the roof of their house was fastened securely, and raised two of the wood sides that gave them extra protection. For a while she worked on her notes again, watched some television, then got ready for bed.

Though she felt tired when she crawled between the sheets, she couldn't sleep. Rain battered the window. Lightning flashed weird shadows on her walls. She tossed and turned uneasily, wondering how large the blob would have grown by the following Wednesday.

Chapter Twelve

Adrienne's palms were sweating as she climbed the stairs toward the lab. She was conscious of Tuck beside her. They hadn't spoken much on the way to school this morning. Today was Wednesday, four weeks into the class.

She knew Brad wasn't there yet, because the janitor had let her and Tuck in the main door. But she didn't doubt that he and probably Shelley also would be along any minute.

Adrienne tried to keep her hand still as she inserted the key in the door. How big? How big? beat her pulse.

Tuck was on her heels as they crossed the room.

"Get the bucket, Adrienne," he said.

She ignored him as she peered through the glass on the side of the aquarium. The blob was now the size of a cantaloupe. Excitement raced through her as she saw how much thinner the gelatinous mass appeared and how much larger the blue shadow inside was. A few times she saw the outside of the blob twitch as the blue form moved. Had Tuck noticed? No. He and the others had only been concerned with outside dimensions. They hadn't studied the blob the way she had, observed its very shape both interior and exterior. She had to put them off a while longer. Then they would see their panic had been for nothing. Impossible as it seemed, she was almost certain she was right.

"Adrienne, you haven't heard a word I said." Tuck took her arm and pulled her around to face him.

"What's going on now?" Brad and Shelley entered the lab together. "Let's see it, Adrienne," said Brad.

She stepped aside far enough for the other two to observe the latest change.

"You have to decide now what you're going to do with that thing," said Brad. "I could take half and you could take half, and we'll do a complete dissection."

"No! I told you I wouldn't let you kill it," said Adrienne.

"Adrienne's right," said Tuck. "The problem is that we've moved it from the swamp. There, it would be in its natural environment. I'll take it back now."

"No!" Adrienne almost shouted the word. "Please," she added softly as she turned a pleading look in Tuck's direction. "Not yet."

"You've decided to call Mr. Garrison?" asked Shelley. She clung to Brad's arm and avoided looking at the aquarium.

"I don't want any of you to touch it. I need more time."

"More time? You've had plenty of time. You've seen what's been happening, Adrienne," said Brad.

"And I told you that you'd have to make a decision today," said Tuck.

"I will make a decision. But I need time." They were closing in on her. She couldn't even count on Tuck to back her up.

"When?" asked Brad.

"Tomorrow. I'll make a definite decision as to what we'll do with the blob tomorrow. One more day, that's all I ask." It couldn't grow much more could it?

"Mr. Garrison will be back from vacation this weekend," said Shelley, "so you won't have any more time after that."

"What do you mean I won't have any more time?" Adrienne asked.

Shelley stepped back and half hid behind Brad. "I mean I called him last week when Brad told me how much the thing had grown. If you weren't going to tell him, I decided I would. But his answering machine said he was on vacation until this Saturday. I said I'd call back then.''

"Shelley Warner, you have a lot of nerve! Who gave you the right to call Mr. Garrison? You aren't even enrolled in this class!'' Shelley, who was once her best friend and had never liked making decisions, had gone behind her back. She hadn't even called and asked if it was all right. "You're a first-class buttinsky.''

"How juvenile to call names,'' said Shelley.

"How juvenile to run to teacher and tattle just because of something different that you can't understand or appreciate.''

"Back off, Adrienne. You've had time to call him yourself,'' said Brad. "Shelley called in exchange for a promise from me not to kill the thing until Mr. G. saw it. She was doing you a favor.''

"I don't want any favors from you two. The blob is my responsibility.''

"Then take that responsibility, and we'll return it where it came from,'' said Tuck.

"Not yet.'' Why couldn't they be patient and trust her? She was willing to take the responsibility for whatever happened. But she didn't want to kill or move the blob.

Should she tell them her suspicions? Would they be more willing to go along with her if she did? Even if she were one hundred percent sure, could she count on them to agree with her viewpoint? She doubted it. Brad might still want to kill it. Shelley would blab about it all over town. Even Tuck might stick to his original idea of returning it to the swamp. In no way could she tell them now what she had guessed might happen when the blob stopped growing, even though she was fairly certain it would, though she didn't know when. She could only plead for more time. Each day counted.

"Mr. Garrison had every right to know about that thing," said Shelley. "This is his class. The assignment to study swamp life came from him. You have no business protecting that yucky blob, Adie."

"I do," said Adrienne. "I found it."

"We were there," said Brad. "I should have dissected it a long time ago."

"This is getting us nowhere," said Tuck, "and I have to go to my class in a minute."

"So go," said Brad. "You don't have any say anyway."

"I have as much say as Shelley or anyone else," said Tuck.

"You'll do whatever Adrienne wants," said Shelley.

"I don't know where you got that idea. You've heard me say I want to take it back to the swamp. I haven't changed my mind about that. We should have talked about this before. Whether Adrienne realizes it or not, we are all in this together. But we didn't talk before, although she's known that she'll have to make a decision about what to do with the thing. I think it would be fair to let her have one more day. Tomorrow, we'll expect that decision. All right, Adrienne?"

"Well, I still think Mr. Garrison has to know," said Shelley.

"Maybe Adrienne will agree with you. That will give her a couple more days. Because she's going to have to choose between our three alternatives. And your idea would give her the most time, Shelley," said Tuck.

"I'll give you my decision tomorrow," said Adrienne. "Now I have work to do."

"Brad, I'm going outside," Shelley said. "I can't stand to stay in here with that thing."

"Go on. I don't have much to do, and I have some errands to run. I'll be finished here in about an hour."

"I'll be back after class," said Tuck.

Adrienne nodded. She didn't look at any of them, not even Tuck. What was she going to do? Brad's suggestion was completely out of the question. Either Shelley's or Tuck's idea was a possibility. But which? She didn't know which would be the best for her or for the blob. She'd have to do a lot of thinking.

Adrienne worked on some soil samples and recorded the progress of the tadpoles until Brad had finished his analysis for the day and cleared off his equipment.

"Tomorrow," he said, as he picked up his notebook. "and don't think of not showing up. If you're not here, I'll make my own decision, and you know what that will be."

"Shut up, Brad."

He tapped the aquarium as he passed. "Your days are numbered," he said.

Adrienne felt sick. So close to knowing, but was she close enough? She didn't know.

She went to the lab door and looked out. No sign of Brad or Shelley. She picked up the bucket. She could put the blob in that to weigh it; but how was she going to get it out of the aquarium? She searched the room for something large enough to hold the cantaloupe-sized thing. There was nothing. "I can almost guess how much larger and heavier you are," she said to the green mass. Several tiny movements rippled across its surface. "I won't disturb you now. Maybe tomorrow. . . ."

She took a surface measurement and recorded the information in her notebook. Then she carried the strong light to the aquarium and set it up behind the glass. She wasn't sure this would work, but she had to check.

As the rays penetrated the gelatin, Adrienne stooped down to peer at the dark shadow better outlined now. "I don't know what you are," she said, "but I have to find out." She snapped off the light, then put it away.

Turning to the water, she analyzed some samples from the aquarium, comparing these analyses to those she'd done on the water before it was added. She took some samples of recently collected water and analyzed those, then added them to the aquarium water. "There you go," she said.

"Are you talking to that thing now?" Tuck closed the lab door behind him.

"I thought you were in class."

"I stayed long enough to hand in my assignment and find out when the next test is. I don't want to listen to the rest of Mrs. Stevens's lecture."

"And I don't want to listen to your lecture," said Adrienne, leading him away from the aquarium.

"You should. Some things have to be said."

"There's nothing you can say that will help," said Adrienne.

Tuck sighed. "I told you I'd take you to the swamp every day. What more could you want?"

"I could want everyone to leave it alone and leave me alone at least until the six weeks are up."

"I can see which direction you're leaning."

"What do you mean?" Adrienne put the scale in the cupboard and wiped the table clean.

"You'll go with Shelley's idea to call Mr. Garrison. You'll buy time. But not much."

"I haven't decided anything definitely."

"Are you ready to go? We'll eat lunch at the mall if you want."

"I'd prefer that you took me home, Tuck. I have a lot to think about—and I think you'd better let me think alone."

She couldn't read the expression on his face. "Sure, chick," he said. "Whatever you say."

"I don't like that term," said Adrienne. "You haven't used it since the first night we went out. I thought it was part of your act."

Tuck shrugged. "It's a word. Mrs. S. says words are good."

"They're not always good, and they can change a lot of things," said Adrienne.

"Like us?"

"I don't know," said Adrienne softly.

"After tomorrow, I'm afraid I do." Tuck held the door open for her.

She double-checked to be sure that it locked behind them. They didn't speak on the way down the stairs or during the ride home. She kissed him on the cheek before getting out of the car and waved as he pulled away.

A few tears slipped down Adrienne's cheeks as she went inside and hurried to the elevator. Was Tuck right? After tomorrow would everything change? After she made her decision, would her wonderful summer be over? She twisted the ring on her finger.

In the kitchen Adrienne found a strainer that looked as if it would be large enough to scoop the blob from the aquarium for at least one more examination.

Chapter Thirteen

After their argument of the day before, Adrienne hadn't really known whether or not Tuck would be picking her up for class. Standing by the balcony rail, she was relieved to see his old Pontiac chug to a stop at the curb.

In a few minutes the front buzzer sounded.

"I'll get it, Mom," she called.

"I'm not up," her mother answered in a sleep-sounding voice. "Tell Tucker I said hello. Oh, and honey, I won't be here when you get back. There's a sale at the mall. I want to be there when the stores open, and I'll shop through lunch hour, then go on to work from there."

"That's all right, Mom. See you later." She went to answer the door.

"Good morning," said Tuck. He looked almost as tired as Adrienne. "Sorry I'm late. Tad is sick, and I had to help my mother with him."

"Nothing serious, I hope."

"She's taking him to the doctor, but I think it's just a summer cold. Have you decided what to do about the blob?"

"I couldn't sleep thinking about it."

"But have you decided?" he repeated, as she closed the apartment door behind them.

"I need more time, Tuck."

He punched the elevator button and turned to face her. "Adrienne, you don't have more time. You were lucky to have until today."

"I need until at least next Wednesday." She didn't look at Tuck as she spoke, pretending to be interested in the swirling pattern of the hallway carpet.

"Don't expect to get it. I might give in just because I love you. But you know that neither Brad nor Shelley will. Brad's determined and Shelley is scared."

"She doesn't have to be and him—well, I don't trust him." The elevator doors slid open and they stepped inside. "Maybe we can talk them into waiting just a few more days?"

"Adrienne, you're postponing the inevitable."

"You're sure learning a lot of big words." She tried to joke, but her comment and the laugh that followed sounded phony and strained.

"Don't change the subject."

They stepped off the elevator and hurried out to the car. Adrienne stared out the side window as they drove toward the campus, but she saw little of the passing scenery. Why couldn't anyone understand? Why was a beach-ball-sized blob so much more threatening than a cantaloupe-sized blob? The lab door was open, and Brad and Shelley were waiting when they got there.

"All right, you two. Explain," Brad demanded. He stood with his arms folded across his chest, reminding Adrienne of the man on the front of the cleaning product her mother used.

"Explain what?" asked Adrienne. She walked across the room toward them. The aquarium bubbled behind Brad and Shelley.

Brad stepped aside.

Adrienne looked and hesitated only a second. "It's gone!" she cried.

"Good observation," said Brad. "Now the big question. What did you two do with it?"

"Us?! You've got that wrong." Tuck peered over Adrienne's shoulder into the aquarium. "All right, Ferris, your turn to talk. Is this your idea of a joke?" He put his arm around Adrienne. "Because it's not funny."

"He said he'd kill it." Adrienne looked at the few inches of empty green water that bubbled in the bottom of the tank. "Is that why you came so early?"

"That's a pack of lies," said Brad. "We weren't any earlier than usual. Ask Shelley. If I had killed it, do you think I'd wait around for you?"

"Yes," said Tuck.

"She'd cover for you." Adrienne glanced at Shelley.

"I wouldn't. And he didn't. The aquarium was empty when we got here. And you didn't seem all that surprised, Adie. We know you and Tuck took that—that thing," Shelley said. The disgust she felt for the blob was evident in her voice.

"Says who? We just got here," Tuck said.

"Later than usual," said Brad. "You didn't rush this morning, did you?"

"And you were the last to leave yesterday," said Shelley.

Adrienne stared at the empty tank. "It's not here, is it?" Her voice shook slightly. She couldn't look at Tuck.

"Adrienne, you don't think that I . . . ?" he began.

"It's gone," she said, this time glancing at him for a second.

His face was flushed. "You know darned well I didn't touch it."

"Of course she does because she was with you," said Brad. "You wanted it to go back to the swamp, Michaels."

"I was not with him," said Adrienne. "I'm the one who wanted you to leave the blob alone. I'm the one who wanted it left here for study. Why would I take it to the swamp?"

"Maybe Mr. Garrison got your message early, Shelley," said Tuck, his voice sounding strained. "Maybe he came in last night and took it."

"That could be what happened," said Brad slowly.

"Do you think so?" Shelley asked.

Adrienne didn't say anything. She continued to stare at the empty tank.

"Cheer up, Adrienne," said Brad. "Now you don't have to make a decision."

"Drop dead," said Adrienne.

Tuck put his arm around her shoulders. "Maybe this is for the best," he said. "Maybe it evaporated or disappeared on its own."

"Come off it, Michaels," said Brad. "On its own? No way. someone had a hand in this. I'd like to think it was Mr. Garrison. That's what I'd *like* to think." His eyes narrowed. He went to his work table and sat on one of the stools, facing them. Shelley followed him.

"None of you wanted it here." Adrienne spit the words out. "Now you've got your wish."

"Michaels felt that way, too," said Brad.

"Ferris, don't point a finger at me," said Tuck.

"Hey, I thought we decided that Mr. Garrison took it." Shelley sounded confused.

"We said he *might* have," said Brad.

"If he did, where is he?" asked Tuck.

Shelley shrugged. She looked at Brad, who shook his head.

"Well, I guess you're all happy now," said Adrienne quietly. She reached over and unplugged the small motor that pumped oxygen into the water. She turned to Tuck. "Are you staying for your class?"

"I should. I've got a quiz. Why?"

"Because I don't feel like working today. I'm going home. I'll take the bus." She walked toward the door.

"Hey, Adie," called Shelley, "what did you decide?"

Adrienne didn't turn to look at her. "It doesn't matter now, does it?" she asked.

Tuck caught up with her. "You don't really believe that I took it?" he asked. Their footsteps echoed in the quiet hall.

Adrienne didn't answer.

They passed Mrs. Stevens's room. Her voice could be heard faintly through the closed door, as she gave directions for the quiz.

"Come on." Tuck took Adrienne's arm.

"You have class. Hurry. Mrs. Stevens is handing out the tests."

"So I'll miss one quiz."

"Tuck, you can't." She wanted to push him through the doorway into his class.

"Yes, I can. I'll make it up." He didn't let go of her arm until they got to the car.

"I said I'd take the bus. Go back."

"The bus doesn't go out to Indian Vale. I'll prove I didn't take that thing, Adrienne."

"Tuck, you don't have to do this. I'd rather go home."

"Yes, I do. I'll take you home after." He started the car. The tires squealed as he backed the car out and raced across the lot and into the street.

"Slow down." She wished he'd just drive her home. But she guessed there was no arguing with him now. He had to show her. She put a hand on the dashboard.

"In a minute." He glanced in the rear view mirror. "Someone else didn't believe me, either," he said.

"What do you mean?"

"Brad and Shelley just jumped into his car. They're following us."

Adrienne glanced back. "Oh, great," she muttered.

"It doesn't matter," said Tuck. "They won't see anything at the swamp, either." He accelerated around a corner and Adrienne slid against him.

The road leading to the marsh was muddy, but Tuck didn't seem to care. He took Adrienne's hand and pulled her along, kicking beer cans out of his path and sending birds flying from their homes in the brush. She was out of breath when they reached the small paths.

Without hesitation, he took the right hand path to the swamp. "Look around," he said, waving an arm at the brackish water. "Do you see it? It's so big you couldn't miss it now. Look everywhere. Look as long as you like. I have all day. I'll wait."

"It's not that big," said Adrienne.

"Big enough not to get lost," said Tuck. "Do you see it? Do you?" His dark eyes flashed.

Adrienne shook her head. She swallowed back tears.

"Now we'll look on the other side." Tuck grabbed her hand again and dragged her back to the road and over to the left hand path.

"Wait, you two," shouted Brad. He and Shelley ran toward them.

"Follow us if you want. You won't see anything, either," Tuck shouted. He dragged Adrienne down the left hand path, through muck and waist high weeds. When they reached the swamp again, he said the same thing. "Do you see it?"

She stared at the still, green water and shook her head.

Tuck passed Brad and Shelley, pulling Adrienne along with him. "Let's get out of here," he said.

"We're going to keep looking," Brad shouted after them.

"Be my guest," answered Tuck.

Adrienne noticed that his jaw was clenched. She had to run to keep up with him. She wished she could tell him that she believed him.

"Now, do you believe me?" he asked, when they were in the car.

"I want to say I do," she said softly.

Tuck swore. He started the car.

Adrienne held on as he raced back the way they'd come. He passed the school, and a short while later the car screeched to a halt in front of her apartment house. He reached across her and opened the door.

"I thought people who loved each other also trusted each other," said Tuck. His eyes looked as shiny as she knew her own must look. "I guess I was wrong. Goodbye, Adrienne."

She stepped onto the curb and closed the door. She could feel the tears spring to her eyes. Had she gone too far? Yet, she'd had no choice. Brad and Shelley had heard Tuck say he thought the blob should go back where it came from. Yet, she knew he didn't take it. She'd tell him she believed him. "Tuck," she said.

He gunned the motor and drove away.

Now tears ran in quick rivers down her cheeks. Keeping her head down, Adrienne dashed through the apartment-house doorway. She didn't wait for the elevator, but went for the stairs. Sobbing half-aloud, she kept running until she reached her floor. She was glad her mother wasn't home. There was too much to explain, and she'd have to do that soon enough. The key stuck in the door. Finally it turned, and Adrienne flung the door open. "I'm sorry, Tuck," she sobbed. "I'm sorry." She ran into her room and threw herself across her bed.

Tweetledum squawked and flapped around in his cage. Lancelot rustled the papers in the bottom of his cage. On the table, her aquarium bubbled softly.

Adrienne glanced up once, then buried her face in her pillow and continued to cry.

Chapter Fourteen

Honey aren't you feeling well?" Adrienne's mother smoothed her hair back from her forehead.

Adrienne caught her hand. "I'm all right, Mom."

"I haven't seen Tuck around. Did you have a disagreement?"

Adrienne stirred her soggy cereal. "Sort of," she said.

"Try to patch things up, honey. He's a nice boy."

"I know, Mom." Adrienne went to the sink and poured the cereal down the drain. "Maybe when my class is over..."

"Your class? What's it got to do with your class?"

"It's a long story, Mom, I don't feel much like talking."

"Marcy, one of the waitresses from work, and I are going to a show this afternoon. Would you like to come?"

Adrienne shook her head. "Thanks, anyway. Um, Mom, I'm rearranging my room, so don't try to go in there. Okay?"

"Keeping busy will only work so long. I speak from experience. You have to call Tucker and talk to him."

"I know. Does that mean I don't have to clean my room?" Adrienne forced herself to smile and speak lightly.

"You know I didn't mean that. If you're going to keep the animals in this apartment, you must take care of them. That means clean cages and clean aquarium and clean room. I suppose they all need doing again. And did you vacuum the bird seed off the carpet? That bird is so messy."

"Not yet. I'll take care of everything, Mom. Promise."

"See that you do. I don't have time to check. I have a hair appointment right now." Her mother pushed her chair back from the table.

Adrienne forced down a half glass of orange juice. "I have to hurry, too. I'll miss the bus."

"And talk to Tucker," her mother reminded her again.

"All right, Mom!" Under her breath, Adrienne whispered, "Stop nagging. I can't stand much more."

She missed Tuck intensely. If only her mother knew how many times she'd reached for the phone to call him! And now she no longer had Shelley to tell her troubles to. She was alone. Very alone.

She took a quick shower, avoided looking at herself in the mirror where she knew she'd see dark circles beneath her eyes and a pale face with no smile. She slipped into jeans and a blue-striped T-shirt.

She glanced around her room. Maybe she would rearrange it one more time, if she had the energy.

She picked up her biology notebook and closed the door behind her. "I'm going, Mom," she called.

"Don't forget to talk to Tuck."

Adrienne clenched her teeth. "See you later," she answered.

She sat in the front of the bus and stood up before the school stop. When the vehicle had deposited her in front of Pendleton High, she stood there for a minute. She had to force her feet to carry her toward the building. No matter how determined she was not to look toward the parking lot, each day her head turned by itself and sought out the beat-up Pontiac. Tuck was going to class every day. She wondered what Mrs. Stevens thought. Had he told her that he'd quit his job? And each day she knew that he sat in his car after classes were over and waited until she walked past the parking lot to the bus stop before he started the motor and drove away. What was he thinking? Did he ever want to call her, too? Could he understand?

She wiped the back of her hand across her eyes, then pushed her hair out of her face, so that any observer would think they were one motion.

Today when she climbed the stairs, she didn't rush, but took each step as if it were a mountain side.

She'd been tempted to give Brad the other key to the lab, but had changed her mind. Would he turn in his duplicate? she wondered. Often she caught him looking at her quizzically. What was he thinking? Was he worried that she'd mention the key to Mr. Garrison?

Shelley was sitting on the end of one of the lab tables swinging her feet and reading a paperback book. She looked up when Adrienne entered. "Guess what?" she asked.

"What?" Adrienne answered automatically. She took the balance out of the cupboard and set it up on the table. From the counter she took her last jar of swamp water.

"Mr. Garrison called me back last night."

Adrienne almost dropped the jar. She set it down and looked at Shelley. "And?"

"And?" echoed Brad. "Why didn't you tell me?"

"I wanted to wait for Adie to come."

"So she's here. What did he say?"

"What did you say?" Adrienne asked.

"Wait a minute and I'll tell both of you. It's too bad Tuck isn't here to listen."

"Count your blessings," said Brad.

Adrienne bit her tongue to keep from saying something back. "Shelley, tell us what Mr. Garrison said."

Shelley smiled. "He said he had a nice vacation and that he'd be here next week."

"Shelley!" Brad yelled.

"What?" She sounded irritated. Weren't things going well between them? Adrienne wondered.

"What did he say about the blob?" Brad demanded.

"Oh that old thing. I didn't mention it."

"Why not?" growled Brad. "That was stupid."

"It was not! The blob is gone; and if he didn't take it, how would I explain what it was and what it looked like? He might think I was a looney or playing a practical joke on him. So I said I'd called to ask if I could take his independent study class next year. And he said he'd see. I told him how interesting I thought it was, and how I'd been watching you two work all this time."

Adrienne unscrewed the cap from her bottle of water. She poured some in the beaker.

"Well, aren't you going to say anything, Adie?" asked Shelley.

"There is nothing to say, Shelley. I'm glad you didn't ask him, but that doesn't change the fact that the blob isn't here where I can finish my experiments."

"I know. I'm kind of sorry I called him, Adie. But I'm not sorry the blob is gone. I had bad dreams about that thing."

"I think you were dumb, Shelley. You could have found out if Mr. Garrison had it," Brad said. "You could have asked him if any of his classes found anything unusual. The way he answered would have given you a clue."

"Mr. Garrison is too smart to give clues," said Shelley, "and I'm tired of you calling me dumb, Brad Ferris."

"Big deal."

Adrienne tried to concentrate on her work.

"Adie, are you going to be home later?" Shelley asked.

Adrienne slopped some of the water out of the beaker. "Sometime later," she said. "I don't know exactly when."

"Good. I'll call you. We have a lot to talk about."

"All right, Shelley," she said. "Make it around dinner time, okay?"

Shelley nodded and slid off the table. "I'm going to the mall."

Brad didn't even look up when she left.

Adrienne sighed. This whole summer had been a mixup. What would happen next week when summer school was over? She put the beaker on the scale and made several notes in her book. A vision of Tuck lounging in the classroom doorway was so strong, that she looked in that direction. But there was no one there. Wishful thinking, she decided. Maybe she and Shelley had both gone full circle where boys were concerned.

If the blob were still here things wouldn't be so quiet, she thought. They'd be gathered around the aquarium looking at the bulging, quivering mass that filled the square from glass to glass. And they'd all be talking about it.

But the blob wasn't there. Only the empty aquarium remained as a reminder. She put her pencil down and went to the counter where it sat.

"What are you doing?" asked Brad.

"Cleaning this out and putting it away. We won't need it anymore."

"True. I was thinking about what Shelley said about making Mr. Garrison believe her. But there is proof."

"Really? What?" asked Adrienne. She rubbed paper towels across the inside of the glass.

"That slide you made. Where is it?"

"At home with my leaf samples. Why?"

"Bring it in next week. We can ask him to look at it and tell us what it is."

"That won't do any good," said Adrienne. She gave attention to the outside of the glass, then stooped to open the cupboard.

"Why not?" asked Brad. "Did you break the slide?"

Adrienne pushed the aquarium onto the shelf and let the door bang shut. She brushed her hands together and turned to face him. "No. But the scraping dried up and fell off. The slide is blank."

Brad frowned. "How do I know you're not lying?"

Adrienne forced a smile. "You don't. And I never know if you're lying, either. So we're even, aren't we?"

Brad turned back to his work, and so did she. In her last soil sample she'd found an interesting fungus sample. She didn't tell Brad. She wrote two pages of notes as she peered into the microscope, observed, then recorded.

When Adrienne had finished, she cleaned up her table, rinsed her bottles and jars, put them in her bucket, checked to be sure that everything was put away where it belonged, and picked up her notebook. "You can lock up," she said. "I'm finished."

"Do you want to compare notes?" Brad asked.

For a minute Adrienne was startled. Then she smiled. "No. But if you're wondering if I'm going to include my study of the blob, the answer is no. I can't show it to Mr. Garrison, so I've decided to leave any mention of it out. See you next week, Brad. I've finished my study. I'll write my report at home."

"Yeah. Listen, tell Shelley I'll call her this weekend."

"Tell her yourself." Adrienne didn't look back as she walked out of the lab.

Chapter Fifteen

At exactly seven-fifteen Adrienne reached for the alarm clock shrilling on the table beside her bed. She yawned, then glanced across the room.

"Ohmygosh," she said and half fell, half jumped out of bed. She stumbled across the room. "Oh wow!" The words were more like a long, drawn out sigh.

She stared into her aquarium for a minute, then lifted the phone receiver. Her heart raced and her finger shook as she dialed. "Tuck?"

"Hmm?" He sounded sleepy. "Adrienne, is that you? Are you all right?"

"Of course I'm all right." She kept her voice low, so she wouldn't wake her mother.

"Can you come over?" she asked.

"Now?"

"Soon. Please?"

"*It hatched.*"

For a minute Adrienne didn't say anything. "What?" She tried to keep her voice normal.

"Did the green thing hatch?" asked Tuck, sounding more wide awake now.

"How did you...? I mean, I don't know what you mean."

"Adrienne, I know you. Just answer yes or no. Did it hatch?"

"Yes."

"When?"

"Last night or early this morning."

"What is it? How does it...? I'll be right there!"

Adrienne hung up and she turned to the aquarium again. Her poor little platys were all crowded into an old fish bowl she'd put on the floor under the table. In their place swam a small blue creature, about the size of her hand. It reminded her of the pictures she'd seen in books about dinosaurs. The shape of the head and the slender neck and the tail were similar. But was it in its final stage? Or like a frog would it change still? Would arms and legs poke out from the blue green skin? And how large would it grow?

The remains of what had been the green blob, the gelatinous mass that had served as an expanding egg, hung like an empty balloon in one corner of the aquarium. The small animal nudged it, then began to nibble at one side.

Quickly Adrienne tore a piece from the gelatinous shell and scooped a small cup of swamp water from the aquarium to put it in. Soon there would be no evidence left. Had she made a mistake by not consulting a biologist when she'd first suspected the truth about her discovery?

And there were other questions. Was this a new animal? She wasn't sure. Dinosaurs had hatched from eggs with shells, at least scientists thought they did. Yet, if some had hatched like the frog, from a gelatinous mass, the evidence would be gone. They wouldn't know, would they? Further, the blob had expanded unlike any kind of egg—frog or turtle. She may have witnessed a whole new birth process.

Her brain felt charged with the importance of her discovery.

More questions. Where had it come from? Were there others? Why had it come? Were there answers?

She hurried to get dressed, making herself beautiful for Tuck. How long had he suspected? Had he kept quiet on purpose? Could he forgive her for not telling him and worse for letting Brad and Shelley accuse him so no one would suspect her?

This would be a day for questions, she thought. And, she hoped, a day for recommitment and love. It would also be a day for decisions, important decisions she could no longer put off. This was a discovery that would have to be shared. She had to decide how and with whom. She did know one thing for sure: this time she wanted Tuck to be with her and to help her.

Delivered right to your door will be heart-felt romance novels by the finest authors in the field, including Diana Palmer, Brittany Young, Rita Rainville, and many others.

You will also get absolutely FREE, a copy of the Silhouette Books Newsletter with every shipment. Each lively issue is filled with news about upcoming books, interviews with your favorite authors, even their favorite recipes.

When you take advantage of this offer, you'll be sure not to miss a single one of the wonderful reading adventures only Silhouette Romance novels can provide.

To get your 4 FREE books, fill out and return the coupon today!

This offer not available in Canada.

Silhouette ❀ *Romance*®

Silhouette Books, 120 Brighton Rd., P.O. Box 5084, Clifton, NJ 07015-5084

First Love from Silhouette

DON'T MISS THESE FOUR TITLES— AVAILABLE THIS MONTH . . .

SOMEONE ELSE Becky Stuart
A Kellogg and Carey Story

When Carey's New York neighbor vanished overnight, Kellogg and Theodore joined in the search. This led them to some unexpected conclusions.

ADRIENNE AND THE BLOB
Judith Enderle

What in the world was Adrienne going to do about the blob? Only Tuck thought he knew, and he wasn't about to tell.

BLACKBIRD KEEP
Candice Ransom

Holly knew at once that she never should have agreed to visit her uncle. His house was too spooky and its inhabitants even weirder. Would Kyle help her to unravel the mystery, or was he working against her?

DAUGHTER OF THE MOON
Lynn Carlock

From childhood, Mauveen had known that somehow she was "different." Should she listen to the ancient ancestral voices, or should she follow the promptings of her newly awakened heart?

WATCH FOR THESE TITLES FROM FIRST LOVE COMING NEXT MONTH

A DAY IN SEPTEMBER
Joyce Davies

"Seize the opportunity," Kim's horoscope had advised her. But first she knew that she had to put Kevin out of her mind and heart—at least that was the way it looked to her early that September morning.

A BROKEN BOW
Martha Humphreys

Dawn was haunted by her unknown heritage. Only Harry, her enigmatic neighbor, could help her, but could she believe the answers she read in his dark eyes?

THE WILD ONE
Tessa Kay

When Beth first glimpsed Con glowering by the cottage door, she knew she had found a modern Heathcliff. Did he recognize her as his Cathy?

ALL AT SEA
Miriam Morton

Casey loved the idea of working on an underwater project with Devlin. He was most definitely a deep-sea treasure! But first she had to fathom his negative attitude.

First Love from Silhouette